SOMETIMES LOVE STINKS

I0617750

By

C. A. King

Cover Design:

JUST WRITE CREATIONS

Editor:

J.D. Cunegan

If you believe this book is dedicated to you,

perhaps it is!

Cover Design: **Just Write Creations**

First Printing: December 2018

ISBN: 978-1-988301-66-2

Kings Toe Publishing

kingstoepublishing@gmail.com

Brantford, Ontario. Canada

Chapter One

In certain cases, fear was considered a wisdom that, when heeded, resulted in survival if one came face to face with danger. Then again, it was also an irrational emotion that tended to cause a total loss of logical thought. Be that as it may, there was one correlation between the types... every person experienced fear in one way or another. There was no avoiding that part, whether from dying, germs, or even heights. None of those phobias, however, mattered to Gastrella. Even monsters, horror movies and clowns, while they weren't on her list of favourite things, never bothered her enough to make her shake in terror. What scared her the most was being made fun of.

In the greater scheme of things, first impressions didn't always play fair. It only took a single brief moment for a mental image to be formed, strong enough to follow and greatly impact the way a person was treated. When that one defining instance happened in the delivery room, it lasted for a lifetime. That was Gastrella's story summed up in a nutshell and there wasn't a thing she could do to change it.

Sitting on the city bus, her attention focused on all the cars zipping by, hoping one of them would calm the bundle of nerves growing in her midsection. Closed-in spaces, especially crowded ones, were the worst for her anxiety. In any vehicle, there was no way to discreetly squeak out some wind. Someone was sure to notice if she did. That meant stares and whispers. Then comments about the smell would circulate, along with the odour. Everyone always knew it was her, too. Once, a passenger complained to the driver about the stench. Without judge or jury, she found herself standing on the corner, excommunicated for the unholy act of farting. The walk home that day had been long-winded in more ways than one.

After that incident, her mother began picking her up. This was the first time since then that she had been left to her own devices; at the worst possible time, too. With all the bags she'd accumulated from shopping, a car ride would have been much easier. Still, the extra work was worth it. Re-inventing one's self, after all, required a new wardrobe.

Gastrella wasn't about to blame her aunt, though. It wasn't as if any woman had a choice about when they went into labour. And it certainly wasn't the baby's fault. He or she wasn't being born to purposefully ruin anyone's plans in particular. If babies possessed the ability to harness the potential they commanded, they could have effortlessly ruled the world.

There was something about a newborn that gave them power over those around them. Every noise a little one made could turn a frown upside down and wipe anger from any mind. They controlled attention.

This little bundle of joy was no different. The whole Balance family was at the hospital waiting on his or her arrival. Gastrella only hoped her aunt and uncle were more sensible naming their child than her parents had been when they named her.

It was hard to be mad at her mother and father. They weren't entirely at fault. Social pressures had a hand in their decision - as they always seemed to. Gastrella was born during one of the peaks in the crazy baby name popularity era. A time when every new parent wanted to outdo the next.

Celebrity couples took the lead, picking the oddest, yet witty names for their new born babies. The whole concept might have been called a fad, if it weren't for the fact it was still going strong in Hollywood.

The story of her defining moment, that first impression that sealed her fate, she had heard a million times. Her mother birthed the perfect pink bouncing baby girl. Excitement and anticipation became a blanket, warming them in the hospital room that day.

When the attending physician turned the babe over, instead of crying, their little bundle of joy let out a blast of methane aimed directly in his face; the stench strong enough to knock him off-balance. The nurse reached the doctor just in time to catch the baby before she hit the floor.

This wasn't the little poof newborns tended to have. This flatulence held the power of a grandfather sitting in a large recliner... one who claimed a mouse under his chair was to blame, but everyone else knew better. No rodent was capable of making such a loud room-vibrating noise or the rotten egg smell that came with it.

The doctor was rushed out of the delivery room, requiring an oxygen mask to recover. They never saw him again. Her parents decided on their child's name right then and there - Gastrella M. Balance.

As a baby, being called Gastrella was cute. If she burped or farted, it was ten times as adorable as other babies. Any other mothers and fathers they met praised them for their unique and appropriate name choice.

Then, as a young child, passing gas was funny. Of course, all kids thought farting was hilarious. In middle school, however, things began to change. By the time she became a teenager, people were offended by the abnormal amount of fumes she released daily. That was when the doctor appointments began.

After a slew of tests it was determined the gas wasn't a product of anything but nerves. She had anxiety - social anxiety, to be exact. Whenever she drew the scrutiny of others, a pain in her stomach began to stir. That was her only warning signal and it was about as effective as a one-minute notice for an incoming twister.

After traditional medicine failed her, she spent most of her free time researching her symptoms and possible remedies. As it turned out, social anxiety manifested in people in numerous different ways. Gas was a normal side effect, although burping or the hiccups were the two more common forms. Aside from that, there were hives, rashes, acne, nausea, vomiting, crying or depression, restlessness, irritability, muscle tension, aches, pains, sweating and a few hundred other things.

In her case, however, knowing wasn't half the battle. There was no way to stop her back-end blowouts, other than to control what triggered them. That was easier thought of than done. Her triggers were other people. Anytime she felt the slightest bit of embarrassment, butt yodelling was sure to follow. That, in turn, aided to the awkwardness, creating a vicious cycle that was hard to break free from. Once teased... always teased.

That was literally why attending a new school was so important. There, no one knew of her issues. She was starting out as just another average student... exactly what she had always wanted to be.

When her father landed a posh job with a new makeup company, they had no choice but to move to Knollville. Spending her senior year of high school in a place no one knew her was a blessing... a chance to start over.

Optimism was an unfamiliar feeling. For the first time, the dread that usually surrounded back-to-school commercials was gone. She was looking forward to the end of summer. This was her chance to be a normal girl for at least one year of her life. She had made a pact with her diary to do just that.

Most of the preparation list had already been crossed off. Her new clothes were in bags around her, ones she picked out, not her parents. The long braids her parents adored had been snipped off, giving way to a shoulder-length cut that framed her oval face in curls. Even details like a manicure and pedicure had been seen to, although she doubted anyone would ever see her toes. This was going to be her year.

Her hand reached up, grabbing the cord to notify the driver that the next stop was hers. Nothing happened. She tugged on it again. A familiar rush of heat filled her cheeks from glares and whispers. Pain struck her midsection. Her breaths became erratic. She pulled hard on the cord one more time, this time summoning a bell, but along with it a roaring from her rear.

The thundering bellow from her butt cheeks sounded more like ripping material than gas. She might as well have torn her pants. There were enough ogles from rubberneckers and gawkers at the back of the bus. Each hoped to catch something embarrassing on camera to share round the dinner table, exchanging giggles over dessert.

"Sorry," she muttered, rushing to the doors as the bus rolled to a jerking stop. She couldn't exit fast enough, hoping no one riding noticed her tooting, or worse went to her new high school.

Chapter Two

If it weren't for Gastrella's name, the Balance family might have been a textbook definition of normal: a mom; a dad; three kids; two cars; and a dog named Brutus. Technically, statistics stated two-point-four kids was the average, but she figured her youngest brother, Chuck, could be counted as the decimal point.

They lived in a two-story, four-bedroom house with a standard two-car garage; the cookie-cutter home the builder had scattered throughout their neighbourhood during construction. That didn't matter, though. What it lacked in originality it made up for in size, being bigger than the one they had before. Here, no one had to share a bedroom.

Thursday nights were family nights in the Balance household. Their once-a-week dinner out was followed by grocery shopping and ended with divvying up food for lunches and snacks. Everyone had their own colour-coded containers, making mornings and afternoons easy to manage. If there was enough time left before bed, they'd pop fresh popcorn for a movie night in. More often than not, though, it was a school night with homework and bed taking precedent over having fun.

"I want tacos!" Todd exclaimed, rubbing his belly. At the age of twelve, he was already as tall as their mother and eating twice as much as their father.

"Mom," Gastrella whined, "he knows I can't eat foods like that. Can't we pick somewhere healthier this week?"

Being second-born, Todd lucked out in more ways than one. First, their parents were over the silly name craze. They had learnt from their mistakes - chosen names didn't always mature well with the children they were given to. Second, he grew up in a completely normal atmosphere with no underlying issues negatively impacting his mental health. Lastly, her brothers, being younger, always got their way.

"Since when is it my fault my sister is a windbag?" Todd argued. "I don't see why the rest of us should suffer because she can't eat good food."

"I'll make you suffer!" Gastrella exclaimed, shaking a fist in the air.

"Yeah," Chuck snorted. "Afterwards... when we can't breathe from all your fumes." He laughed, slapping his knee as his eyes teared up.

"That's not called for!" Mrs. Balance yelled. She turned to her daughter, her voice softening. "They don't mean it, dear."

"Yeah, we do," Chuck blurted out. "She's the lean mean bean machine, farting out gasses until we're all green." He stuck out his tongue. At merely ten years old, he was quick with the one-liners, being able to out-pun anyone, friend or foe. The latter tended to mean he came home with an overabundance of bruises, especially black eyes.

"Okay," Mrs Balance said, "we don't need that. If you can't behave, we won't have dinner out. We'll go home."

"No, we won't," Todd argued. "Then you'd have to cook."

"He's right, sweetheart," Mr. Balance piped up. "You love Thursday nights. We aren't going home. You boys better behave, though. Alright, then... who wants tacos?"

"Mom?!" Gastrella exclaimed.

"I am sure they will have something non-greasy on the menu that you can order," she replied, placing her arm around her daughter's shoulders and adding a squeeze. "It'll be fine."

"You always say that," Gastrella mumbled.

"Well," her mother said, nodding her head, "this time, it will be. You'll see. Restaurants are starting to cater to all sorts of dietary restrictions."

The choices were anything but fine and came with a free side of re-fried bean jokes and wet-fart sauce. Neither of which she wanted. Her brothers were still at an age where they could get away with letting one rip in public. Firing a stink torpedo was a game to them, one they played at every opportunity. What was worse, the stench they created in any restaurant they always blamed on her and usually with the waiter or waitress within earshot.

She was comfortable with her own family enough that, when she did pass gas at home, it was from normal causes.

Everyone did, after all, cut the cheese on a daily basis. When her brothers drew attention to her in public, however, they opened an entirely different wind tunnel.

Restaurants were particularly bad for her. They were small areas that crowded as many tables as close to each other as possible. There was nowhere to hide if one squeaked out of any of her family members, including herself. Someone was bound to hear or smell and know which direction it came from. That was when the finger-pointing competition between Todd and Chuck always began. The winner was decided by the total number of strangers they each convinced of their sister's guilt in connection with the polluted air.

Every week, Gastrella was elated when they finally reached the grocery store. At least there, she could leave a poof in one aisle and hide in the next. No one knew for sure who the culprit was that way. Even her two brothers joined in the game, seeing who could get the best reactions out of clueless shoppers, as they walked through the cloud of foulness they each left behind. That was the best part of family night. The only one left out was poor Brutus.

Gastrella grabbed several boxes of dog treats, handing them off to her younger brothers to sneak into the cart. They could get away with those tactics; she always got caught.

Chapter Three

Gastrella stood staring at the building, backpack slung over one shoulder. Knollville High School was her one chance to have something worth remembering from her teenage years. A grin made its way across her lips. She'd practised meditation and relaxation techniques all summer to help her make it through. As long as nothing extremely embarrassing happened, she was as good as gold. Normal was about to become her new middle name. Not literally, of course; the M initial in her name stood for Madeline.

The hustle and bustle of the first day of school had already begun. Groups of students gathered in cliques outside. She studied each, trying to find a spot where she might fit in. There were four or five skateboarders, doing tricks up and down the stairs; the jocks tossing about a football while girls cheered them on; a group wearing all black recited dark poetry to anyone who would listen; several couples practising tonsil hockey; and the popular girls who would be voted most likely to become famous later in the year.

Just because she didn't fit into one of those groups, didn't mean she wouldn't find one she did. Gastrella took in shallow breaths, not wanting to suck in too much extra air, before heading to the front steps and a new life of possibilities. This was going to be the best day of her existence... she was sure of it.

The office doors were easy to find from the entrance. She stood, back to the counter, watching all the other students filing in and assessing her choice in clothing. The hammer had hit the nail directly on the head. She looked almost exactly the same as anyone else and would blend in easily.

A group of boys from outside walked by, a football flying over heads between them. Each was a portrait of perfection in their own way. She licked her lips, allowing the tiniest of sighs to escape.

"Football team," the girl standing beside her said. "Guess you figured that out from the matching jackets and the pigskin. I'm Molly, by the way." She held out a hand.

Gastrella glanced down at a pair of large brown eyes glaring up at her from under a black fedora-style hat. When she got by that, she realized Molly was overweight. Regret tasted horrible - the second thing she noticed about the girl was her size. How could she expect people to see past her imperfections if she couldn't see past theirs?

"Gastrella," she answered, accepting the girl's offer.

"That's an interesting name," Molly said, nodding.

"Yeah," Gastrella replied. "I'm changing it the minute I turn eighteen. I am literally counting down the days."

"I don't blame you," Molly said. "No offence. You're new here, right? I mean... I haven't seen you around before."

There it was the first of many judgments to come because of her name. "Yes," Gastrella answered, biting her bottom lip. "I was hoping someone would have a map to tell me how to find my classes."

"Maps," Molly said, beginning to look like a bobblehead. "Knollville isn't big on maps. I can help you find your locker and first class, if you want."

A smile graced her lips. "Thank you. I appreciate the offer."

The two headed out into the crowds already littering the hallways. Laughter echoed from one side, although ascertaining who exactly it came from would have been impossible. Almost everyone wore an undeniable smile. Kids might have argued that they hated school, but looking at them that morning was proof it wasn't all bad.

"Your locker is this way," Molly said, glancing over her shoulder to make sure she hadn't lost her new friend. Not that there was a chance of that. Molly had short legs that took two steps or more for every one of Gastrella's own. She stopped and pointed. "Number thirty-three."

"Thanks," Gastrella mumbled, feeling overwhelmed as students banged into her shoulders pushing by. Not one took more than a quick glance in her direction. The bell rang making her jump.

"Your next room is two doors up," Molly said, backing away. "I'll be in the cafeteria at lunch if you need more help or want to talk."

Like magic, the hallways were silenced, void of all life. Gastrella raced for the closing door for her math course, not wanting to be singled out as late. Sitting down, she practiced her breathing exercises. So far, so good. Not a single butt squeak had been heard.

Chapter Four

Gastrella knew lunch would end up being her biggest trial of the day. Regret left a bitter taste in her mouth. The game of hide-and-fart at the store the previous Thursday had lasted a bit too long, cutting into her food selection time. That meant a week of buying meals at school.

She moaned at the size of the line-up and, even worse, the cafeteria's menu. Almost everything listed was bound to cause a stomach problem for one student or another. Her tray landed back in the dwindling pile she'd found it in. A banana and water would suffice, if she ever made it to the front of the queue to pay for them.

Shuffling along in time with the rest of the traffic, she had a bird's eye view of the chow - not that she wanted it. Most of what she saw, she couldn't identify, including the platter the boy in front of her was salivating over. To her, it resembled a plastic hockey puck smothered in a thin brown liquid. Even the side of vegetables were nothing but a mush of colours slopped into a rectangular cardboard bowl.

By the time she'd moved to the cash, the rest of the lunch room was buzzing with activity. Laughter and conversations trumped eating as groups gathered at tables.

"Five dollars," the lunch lady said without so much as a fake grin. Her face remained solemn as if the net over her head had pulled back all emotion along with her hair.

"For a banana and water?" Gastrella questioned with a gasp. Inflation was one thing, but that was highway robbery.

"Five dollars," the woman repeated. "If you don't want it, leave it in that pile." She motioned behind her. "There's a line."

Gastrella pulled a bill from her pocket, handing it over with widened eyes. She had to eat something. A growling stomach was as embarrassing as any other bodily function. Being flustered tended to lead to worse things, too.

She snaked through students and tables, searching for an open spot to take a seat at. There were a few faces from her classes and some of the groups from outside, but none she felt comfortable walking up to. Chomping on her bottom lip, she turned for the door. Stairwells had done her well in the past, that part of her life didn't need to change. Re-inventing one's self required baby steps.

"Hey," Molly said, tapping on the back of her shoulder. "You look lost. You can come sit with us, if you want."

Gastrella nodded, following the girl to a table partially hidden in the back of the room. "Hi," she said, taking a seat.

"They don't talk much," Molly explained. "That's my job. I'm pretty much the spokesperson for everyone here. So going around clockwise, we have Abigail, Tim, Leif, Mitsy, and you know me." She snorted a laugh. "At least, I hope you do." She settled back into her spot, in front of a double order of hockey puck surprise.

Gastrella forced a smile, placing her banana on the table. Water bottle in one hand, her fingers twisted the cap on and off without purpose.

"Where's your lunch?" Abigail asked, glancing up from her book for the first time. "Or are you on a special..." She licked her lips. "Diet?"

"I am on a special diet," Gastrella replied, although she was certain from the girl's red contacts and pasty white makeup that she wasn't referring to being gluten free.

"So am I," Abigail said, adding a deep throaty chuckle on the end. Her fingers played with a tiny vial filled with red liquid hanging from her neck.

"You are going to scare her," Lief commented. "This is why we never make any new friends." He sniffled, wiping his nose with his hand. "I'm Lief." He offered his germs along with a handshake.

Gastrella bit her bottom lip. That wasn't going to happen. "Hi," she said, offering a wave from across the table.

It was Tim who returned the wave, mouthing a *hi* before rolling his eyes and going back to a handheld video game. Mitsy never uttered a word, staring at Gastrella throughout the entire lunch, with the occasional blink thrown in for good measure.

"How is the day going?" Molly asked. "Meet anyone interesting? Dating someone on the football team yet?"

"No," Gastrella replied, giggling. "I doubt that's going to happen." She glanced around the rest of the room. "Does everyone always sit in the same groups?"

"Pretty much," Molly answered between mouthfuls of food. "Knollville High is just like any other school." She nodded at various tables as she spoke. "We have the jocks... meaning the guys who play football; the cheerleaders... they talk in cheers; the female jocks... if you like field hockey; the science club; the metal heads; the goths; the drug addicts and, of course... the witches."

"Witches?' Gastrella questioned.

"Yeah," Molly replied. "See the girl with the blonde ponytails and frilly black dress?" She didn't wait for an answer. "That's Penelope. Her family has lived in Knollville longer than anyone else. The group she's sitting with are all connected to the craft. I've heard they have special rituals and chant spells naked in graveyards." She bit her bottom lip, nodding.

"That's hot," Abigail said, brushing strands of long black hair from her face. "I wanted to be a witch. Apparently, you have to have some sort of power, though." Her shoulders lifted and fell as her eyes reverted back to the charcoal sketching she was working on.

"So what about all of you?" Gastrella asked. "What is this group?"

Every person at the table stopped what they were doing. Their gazes raised to meet the flush filling Gastrella's cheeks. The familiar twang of pain in her midsection made an appearance for the first time that day.

"We don't have one," Molly answered.

"Yeah, we do," Tim argued. "We are the loose ends."

"Loose ends?" Gastrella echoed.

"You know," Lief replied, "the ones who weren't accepted anywhere else and came together because human nature dictates we have some form of social interaction." He scratched his nose, finding a lump under one fingernail. It dug in deep, releasing a white ooze. His sleeve became a tissue once again, adding to the already multiplying germ fest living on his arm.

"Why are you here?" Abigail asked. "There's nothing wrong with you. If you weren't sitting here, I'd peg you for one of the popular girls."

"I-I," Gastrella stuttered, glancing over her shoulder at the group Abigail had nodded towards. Her eyes fixated on one of the boys. He'd been in the group tossing footballs around outside before school. Her stomach swirled, but this time with butterflies.

"I agree," Tim said, following her line of sight. "You belong hanging off of Tanner's arm. That's his name, in case you didn't know."

"Who?!" Gastrella shrieked, her face reaching the glowing point. She clenched her butt cheeks together, hoping nothing would slip out. She'd need an exit soon if this conversation kept up.

"Don't sweat it," Tim replied. "All the girls like Tanner. I can't say I blame them, he's a hottie." A few beeps from his handheld device pulled his attention back.

"I didn't properly introduce you," Molly grimaced. "Guys, this is Gastrella."

Once again, the table stopped all activities to glare in her direction. Even Mitsy's blinking ceased, leaving behind an empty stare.

"That explains it," Abigail said. "Sucks your parents didn't have the wherewithal to give you a better name. You could have been prom queen. It's amazing how much something as simple as a name can change a person's life."

"I don't want to be prom queen," Gastrella squeaked. "I just want a normal year to finish high school, without any controversy."

"Good luck with that," Abigail scoffed.

"Thanks," Gastrella said. "I'll see you later." The building pressure was reaching its maximum holding point. It was a race for the exit. The cool fall breeze whisked away any evidence of the vapour from her nether regions. The crisis had been averted, at least for now. She still had half the day to finish without incident to declare a victory.

Chapter Five

A sigh of relief passed through her slightly parted lips. She'd made it on time, despite taking two wrong turns and completing a full tour of the school. A window seat remained open and was exactly what she needed. The serenity of fluffy clouds against a light blue backdrop always had a calming effect on her nerves.

Winding her way through rows of desks, she ducked under one of several paper planes gliding through the air towards the front of the room. Swinging her backpack off her shoulder, it bumped a student standing behind her.

"Sorry," she mumbled, claiming her seat.

"That's okay," he replied. "You're new here."

Gastrella's heart skipped a beat as she glanced up into the most perfect set of brown eyes. "Yeah," was all she could manage on shaky breath.

"I'm Tanner," he said, flashing a glimpse of his pearly whites from behind a nonchalant grin.

Abigail's words from earlier haunted her memory. Tanner was possibly the best looking guy in existence and he was talking to her. For a brief moment, she was someone. She felt special. All that was bound to crash down around her, sending her back into the world of obscurity and ridicule she called home; it took only one word... her name.

"Hi," she replied, flashing a quick smile before facing forward. If she didn't say it, maybe things would be okay.

"Good afternoon," a man said, entering the room. The door slammed behind him. "I am Professor Jenkins and this is the wonderful world of numbers. This is algebra!"

X equalled saved by the teacher. That was perfect timing. Pulling out a notebook from her backpack, her pencil case dropped on the floor. The first rule of anyone learning how deal with pantie burps was never bend over. She bit her bottom lip, glaring at her pink bag lying in the middle of the aisle. The tiny hearts she'd drawn on it in red ink mocked her, a challenge she wanted desperately to refuse. When she first drew them there hadn't been a person in mind. That was why she left them as outlines. They were more a wish for a boyfriend to call her own. In one day, Tanner had filled in all the blank spots... at least in her mind, he had. He was the dream she secretly wanted to come true.

"It might be the first day," Mr. Jenkins said, "but you will want to start taking notes. This is senior year and none of it will be easy, not even today."

She alternated her glances between the teacher's chalk scribblings beginning to cover a blackboard and her pretty pink case. This was a disaster. With Tanner one desk back and to the left of her, he was sure to notice if she dropped any F-bombs. That would quickly put an end to any hopes for romance. Even if love wasn't in the teacher's equations, she could still fantasize. Her eyes stung at the thought of those dreams being crushed, leaving her empty once again.

"You dropped this," Tanner said, nudging her in the shoulder with the pink case.

"Thanks," she replied, glancing back at his alluring smile.

He brushed his sandy hair to the side with his free hand. "No problem," he whispered, arching his eyebrows suggestively.

She spun back round, facing the front of the room. Chomping on her bottom lip, she desperately tried to conceal sheer joy from attempting to burst free. In a split second, Tanner had changed her life more drastically than he could ever have realized. A smile, a gesture, and a kind word was all it took to make anxiety and depression merely words in the dictionary.

The bell sounded too soon. Lost in her own fantasy, she was almost trampled trying to reach the hallway. She stepped to one side, back against the wall, allowing the traffic to pass. Once the coast was relatively clear, she glanced both ways, deciding which would be the better choice to find her next class.

"Where you headed?" Tanner asked, peeking at her schedule. He moved to stand facing her, tossing a football in the air and catching it while he spoke, showing off a coordination level she had no hopes of ever attaining.

"Room 205E," Gastrella replied.

"English," Tanner said. "I'm headed there too." He pointed. "Three doors down on the left."

A group of boys tackled him from the side, pushing him down the hallway. The football slipped from his grip into that of another senior. He chased after them.

The grin on Gastrella's face reached its maximum width. Not only was she headed to her favourite class, creative writing, but Tanner was going to be there as well. Things were definitely looking up. She followed his instructions to the door, gliding on a wave of happiness the likes of which she'd never felt before.

A blonde girl knocked Gastrella out of the way, whipping gold locks in her face as she passed. "Sorry," she muttered, strutting into the classroom.

A series of whistles followed the girl's movements. As with most stereotypical perfect tens, she came pre-installed with every b in the book: bleach-blonde, blue-eyes, and big-boobs. Even worse, this barbie doll wannabe had taken her place clinging to Tanner's arm.

Gastrella's gaze met his. There was nothing concrete in the simple glance over his shoulder. The way he shrugged the other girl off, however, gave her the hope she needed to stay positive.

With no seats left near her crush, she sat at the back of the room. At least she had a good view of him from there. That was bound to inspire more than one or two lines of creative writing. Those words, however, were better suited for her diary rather than the classroom.

Chapter Six

Gastrella flopped back one her bed, staring at the white stars her father had stuck to her ceiling. Later, when the lights went out, they would glow softly, helping her sleep.

As a young child, their annual family camping trips had been the highlight of every year. Then life became more complicated. When the economy took a turn for the worse, her father found himself standing in the unemployment line. Dollar store stickers replaced expensive trips. It wasn't the same as sleeping under real stars, but it was still special nonetheless. Any father who went out of his way to do a little extra for their child deserved praise. How much money was spent doing it was irrelevant.

Landing this new job in Knollville solved many of their problems. Even with the property values much lower than other places, it was still going to be a long time before an actual vacation was in their futures, though. The glow-in-the-dark shapes appeared a few days after she finished unpacking.

A frilly pink and white pillow found its way into her arms. She buried her face in it, hiding a growing grin. Unable to contain her excitement, her legs began to kick, bouncing up and down on her mattress. The only thing lacking from an otherwise amazing day was someone to share it with. She'd been overly obsessed all day making sure she didn't have any embarrassing moments. A twinge of regret set in for not asking for Molly's phone number.

Being a social butterfly was new to her. In her teenage years she'd never had a best friend, let alone something to share with them. No one wanted to be associated with the gassy girl or the stink that followed her. It was easier to join in the jokes than to stick up for the underdog. Tomorrow was another day and an opportunity to rectify the problem by inviting Molly over after school.

Gastrella tossed the pillow aside, reaching over to her nightstand. Pulling out the drawer, she grabbed the diary hiding within. Her fingers traced the unicorn pictured on the cover, coming to rest on the lock. That small keyhole had been its bodyguard for well over a year now, keeping all of her personal experiences, thoughts, and feelings safely hidden from the rest of the world. One hand forced its way into the tight front pocket of her jeans, emerging with a handful of offerings. A single finger pushed them around in her palm, as she took stock of her treasures. Few were of any real use.

A wrapper that had been refilled with the used gum it came with went straight into the trash container beside her bed. Ever since reading a blog that claimed it was deadly for a bird to eat any of the sticky remains that people tended to spit out, she made sure she properly disposed of it.

The article stated birds mistook the discarded bits for pieces of bread. Once eaten it ruined their systems, stopping them from ingesting proper nutrients. Whether that was true or not didn't matter. She wasn't willing to take any chances. Thoughts of the poor feathered creatures suffering a slow death was too much to handle when it took only a few extra steps for her to toss it in the trash can.

A few pieces of string and lint joined the gum wrapper. That left her with a variety of coins, a lip gloss and one tarnished key. The coins clanged together as they landed on the table beside her alarm clock, the balm joining them. That left the one thing she needed, the key.

It spun around in her fingers before finding its place in the lock. A click sounded from a single turn to the left. The book opened. Its pages fanned out to the exact point she left off the last time she visited, offering her a blank spot to record memories of the past few days. The best part about having a journal as a confident was that it didn't need to be updated daily. In some instances, weeks went by without her writing a single word. It was there, however, whenever she felt the need to express herself.

A pen topped with pink feathers was ready, willing, and able in her grip. Setting it to paper, her hand begin to smoothly slide. She took in a breath of air and puckering her lips as if she were going to whistle, she released it again, writing the first word, *Hey.*

The words *Dear Diary* were a little too corny. If she was going to put her inner most thoughts and feelings into words, they were going to reflect her style, not some preconceived idea of how a diary should be kept.

Today I met the boy I'm going to marry. Of course, he doesn't know it yet. Technically, we did only meet today. He doesn't even know my name. I know that makes things a bit complicated. When I first saw him, I thought I'd be admiring him from the shadows for the entire year. Then the unthinkable happened. He actually noticed me. It wasn't because of a fart, either. He took the time to talk to me like anyone else. For two classes, I felt like a normal girl.

There's still a problem to overcome. I haven't mentioned my name, yet. That could be the deal breaker. Maybe I'll ask Molly to help me figure that part out. Did I mention I made a friend, too? Whatever happens, I'm glad we came to Knollville. I'm hoping to ride this wave as long as possible. Now I know my name is at least half the battle, I am more than ready to have it changed after my next birthday.

Sounds like mom wants me. I'll be back when something else happens. Later gator!

"Gastrella!" Mrs. Balance yelled.

The barking in the background gave away what her mother wanted without any words needed. Brutus was in the yard and his arch nemesis had made an appearance.

"Coming," she answered, locking her diary before stashing it back in the drawer. The tiny key disappeared back into her pocket before heading down.

"Oh, good," Mrs. Balance said, a sigh of relief escaping with the words. "See if you can settle Brutus down. I don't want our new neighbours getting upset. I hate to make waves."

Gastrella slid open the kitchen door. "Brutus," she called. "Come here, boy. Come on. I have some cookies." She shook the box of treats. A pile of fur came bounding through the door, tongue hanging out. "That's a good boy." He snatched the offering from her hand, gulping it back with barely a single chew. He wagged his tail waiting for another treat.

"You know," Mrs. Balance said, "you are rewarding him for bad behaviour. He'll never learn anything that way."

"I am of the opinion that we'll all be grateful he's here when the evil squirrels try to take over the world," Gastrella argued. "There won't be a single one in our neighbourhood. Then the neighbours will be thanking you for having such a brave dog."

"Right," her mother replied, with an eyeroll. "Dinner is in five."

Chapter Seven

Day two was almost as difficult as the previous one had been - the only difference being Gastrella now knew which way to wind or duck to reach the front doors without incident. She even managed to sidestep an out-of-control skateboard. That was an achievement in itself. Coordination was normally a word that only held meaning in fashion in her life. The rule of thumb was if it could be tripped over, it ended up under her feet.

Traversing the halls was as dangerous as walking in a mine field. Between students' legs stretched out on the floor to step over, others walking and locker doors flinging open, it was a wonder anyone made it to class in one piece or without a barrage of bruises.

There were only a few minutes left before the bell rang. Hopes of finding Molly before first period were quickly dwindling. Then she spotted a hat in the crowd. It wasn't the same colour as the day before, but it was the same style. That had to be her. Not everyone could pull off wearing a hat. Molly was one of the lucky few; on her they looked natural.

Gastrella raised her arm, waving over top of heads as she inched closer. A glare froze her on the spot. Her arm lowered. It was the same girl from her English class. The familiar jolt of pain in her midsection coincided with the array of conspiracy theories running through her mind. Molly wasn't the type to hang with the popular girls. She'd said that herself the day before. Yet there they were, chatting away like best friends by the water fountain. The conversation ended abruptly with the blonde walking away.

Gastrella only saw Molly's expression for a second, but that was enough to recognize the anguish she herself had felt for years. Frown lines solidified in place and, before she realized it, a full scowl had taken over her face. It was silly, really. She'd known Molly for all of one day. Why did she feel as if something was wrong? Not everyone smiled twenty-four seven.

The bell rang. Students scurried off to one door or another. The first class of the day was about to begin. There was little choice but to wait for lunch to check on her friend. All she could do was hope Molly was okay until then.

Concentrating on her morning lessons was almost impossible. Guilt overtook reasonable thought. All the times she had been made fun of or needed a kind face, no one had been there. Now, there was a chance the one friend she made needed her and instead of trying to help, she went to class.

There were plenty of excuses. Not dealing with issues had been her whole existence. Keeping her nose in a book studying was easier and made her a straight-A student. What she wasn't familiar with was compassion. No one had ever shown it to her, so how was she expected to show it to someone else?

It didn't matter what arguments she came up with in her own mind. The fact was she was guilty of doing nothing. She'd always wondered why no one stepped in and stood up for her, or even stopped to give the speech about not listening to jerks. The proverbial shoe was on the other foot and it wasn't as comfortable as she had imagined it would be.

Her things were packed before the bell rang. She raced for the door, making it there before any of the other students. The only thing on her mind was making it to the lunch room - to Molly.

Her pulse raced along with her feet. In the rush, it was impossible to be careful. She barely sidestepped some students and bumped into others, all in the name of navigating the sea of teens making their way to the cafeteria. Even with the added quickness, she was the last to arrive at misfit table.

"Hi," Molly said, as if nothing was wrong.

Gastrella took a minute to catch her breath. "Hey." She alternated glances between each of those sitting with her before expanding to the rest of the room. Her eyes settled on Tanner for a moment.

"What's going on with you and Tanner?" Molly asked, a stern look encompassing her round face.

Gastrella gasped, her mouth open. "What?"

"I heard a rumour you two were flirting," Molly said, unwrapping a sandwich. Without waiting for an answer, she took a bite.

"No!" Gastrella shrieked. "I dropped my pencil case and he picked it up. That's it. I don't even know how to flirt."

Molly giggled. "Good," she said. "Keep it that way. Cassidy, the blonde girl, she's been dating him on and off for a while now. You don't want to get on her bad side."

Gastrella glanced back over. "No," she agreed. "Don't worry. I only want an incident-free senior year. Besides, this table and that table probably don't mesh well, right?"

"You got that right," Abigail interrupted. She shrugged her shoulders, then returned to her sketch pad.

"Is that what you two were talking about this morning?" Gastrella asked. "I saw you and Cassidy by the fountain together."

"Yeah," Molly replied. "She wanted me to make sure you knew he was taken. I said I'd pass the message on. Mission completed." She emptied the remainder of the contents of a brown paper bag on the table, picking a brownie as next in line for devouring.

"If you aren't busy later," Gastrella said, "maybe you could come over to my place and hang out after school."

Molly froze, raising only her eyes. "You want to do something outside of school?"

"Yeah," Gastrella answered. "I thought we could watch a movie or something..." Her voice trailed off.

Molly's mouth opened wide, but only air escaped at first. "I can't," she finally said. "It's a school night and I am not allowed to go out." She rolled her eyes, continuing, "My grades last year weren't exactly stellar."

"Yeah," Gastrella replied, "no problem." She gulped back half of a bottle of water, to avoid adding anything else to the conversation. "Maybe on the weekend."

"It's my birthday," Molly blurted out. "You can come over if you want. Nobody will be home but me. I could use the company."

"Is this like a party thing?" Abigail asked. "I don't do parties." Her lips twitched. "Okay, fine... I'll come. Don't expect a present or anything, though."

Molly's face lit up, fireworks exploding in her eyes. "I've never had a party for my birthday before. I mean, I did when I was younger... much younger."

Using a napkin, she provided directions to her house. Mitsy glanced over her shoulder, recording the address on her arm without saying a word.

"We have a pool," Molly stated. "Bring your suits. I'll make sure we have snacks and drinks. This is going to be so much fun."

"Pool?" Lief echoed. "I'm in. The temperature is supposed to skyrocket this weekend one last time. Keeping cool was on the agenda anyways." He nodded as he spoke. "What about you?"

Tim looked up from his game, feeling a nudge in his side. "Yeah, great," he answered. "Text me the address. I'll be there. What systems do you have? I can bring some games."

"Most of them," Molly replied. "We can set them up outside if you want. Don't worry about games; my brother's just collect dust. We can play them."

"Sounds great," Tim admitted. "What time?"

"How about two?" Molly suggested.

Gastrella smiled, agreeing to the time. Maybe she wasn't the only one who needed a friend after all. Maybe there were a lot of people who felt like she did. She didn't have the answers yet, but she was going to her very first high school party. That warranted an entry in her diary later. First, however, she had two more classes to get through. They weren't going to be as much fun knowing Tanner had a beautiful girlfriend, but she still had her dreams, even if she had to keep them to herself.

Mr. Jenkins was already in the classroom with their math work plastered in white all over the blackboard. His beady eyes followed her as she crossed in front of his desk on her way to her seat.

"Wait," he called out.

She froze for a moment before pivoting. "Yes," she answered, biting her bottom lip.

Mr. Jenkins frowned, snapping his fingers and pointing. "Don't tell me," he ordered. "It's on the tip of my tongue." He sighed, glancing down at his sheet of names. His eyes doubled in size. "We'll go with Miss Balance. Is that alright with you?"

"Perfect," she answered.

The remainder of the class flew by, filled with complex equations that even gave star students a run for their money. If she hadn't been top of the class the previous year, she was certain she would have been falling behind in this one.

The bell rang. That left one class to end her second day on a positive note. She waited for the others to leave before heading out the door herself. There was no use stirring the pot. If Tanner had a girlfriend, she wanted to see as little as possible of them together. Gastrella made her way down the hallway to the English room.

"'Hey," Tanner said, coming up behind her.

Gastrella jumped.

"Sorry," he said, smiling. "I wasn't trying to scare you."

"It's fine," Gastrella replied, shaking her head. "I was lost in thought."

"Math will do that to you," Tanner smirked. "That's going to be a nasty course. I never did like math. If it wasn't a requirement, I'd drop it in a flash." He bowed, motioning with one hand. "Our room, my lady."

Gastrella chuckled. "Thank you."

There it was again... hope. Every time she convinced herself she didn't have a chance, he showed up and made it all seem plausible.

"Tanner," Cassidy called out. "I need you."

"Seems I am being beckoned," he said, flashing a wink. "Talk to you later." He slid past her, taking his place on the top level of the hierarchy of her peers.

"Good afternoon," Mr. Tempo said, gliding into the room. "I am handing out your first assignment. You have until Monday to produce a poem."

The room groaned.

"This isn't just any poem, either," the teacher continued. "I want a stack of love sonnets, minimum a dozen lines and fully coherent. I'll be grading this and don't mind if it is longer. In fact, I recommend it is to anyone who would like to pass this course." He paced up and down the aisles.

"What if we aren't in love?" a student named Chuck asked, tossing a football in the air.

Mr. Tempo caught it on the way back down. "Then write about the sport you seem to love so much. You can have this back after class." He raised the football in the air, carrying it back to his desk. "Everyone loves something. Figure out what that is for you and turn it into a composition. I don't care if it is an ode to spaghetti. It needs to be on my desk by the beginning of class Monday."

Chuck groaned, letting out a mouthful of air. "Great," he complained. "Some of us have football practice."

"If you don't have the assignments for my class done," the teacher argued, "some of you won't have to worry about football practice for very long. Maintaining a good grade is a prerequisite to being on the team. Love poetry on my desk by Monday... no exceptions."

Chapter Eight

Her lips curved upwards, forming a grin of satisfaction. A sparkle ignited in her eyes. There was a certain amount of giddiness that accompanied her as Gastrella walked through her own front door. It was Friday and an entire week had passed without any major incidents. She tossed her backpack on the ground, wary of her brothers. Either one of them could have burst in at any time, making her few moments of delirious happiness nothing more than a distant memory. They might have been banned from using paint guns and water pistols in the house, but marshmallow shooters were still in play.

Her eyes shifted from side to side. It wasn't paranoia. Silence meant something was up. Perhaps a trap had been set for her in one room or another. Such was life with two younger brothers. They always had something planned and she usually fell right into their net.

She glanced down at two brown eyes peering out from beneath white and black fur. "Where are they, boy?" she asked.

Brutus was a family pet, but where exactly his allegiance lay when it came to the three siblings was a mystery. He was puppy when they first brought him home, a raw bundle of energy bursting at the seams and a true mutt through and through. Age was catching up to him, but every now and then his puppy spirit came out to play. When that happened, he was as mischievous as her brothers. Of course, in the end, Brutus could be bought for a price of a rawhide bone or pocket full of biscuits.

"Anyone home?" she called out, heading to the kitchen and finding it immaculately clean, but empty. Gastrella had an appreciation for her mother's housekeeping abilities. There weren't many women who could rival her in that department without the help of a professional cleaning service or maid. A note sitting on the counter caught her attention.

Enrolling the boys in martial arts this afternoon. Brutus needs to be walked. Your brothers fed him Fred. He has been having tummy problems since. Take extra bags.

Love, Mom

Gastrella shook her head, not knowing which part of the message was worse; her brothers taking martial arts; them feeding the dog their pet fish; or that Brutus had the runs. She felt him brush up against her feet, before lying down on them with a doggy sigh.

"Let me change and I'll take you for a walk," she moaned, heading up the stairs.

There was no way she was wearing her good clothes for a job like that. A pair of jeans and an old baseball-style shirt over a tank top were more appropriate. She pulled her hair back, tying it with an elastic while taking two steps at a time on the way down. A few locks came loose, forming a frame for her face. Her hair wasn't long enough for a fully ponytail, but rather made a cute bunch of spirals when she wore it that way.

Brutus was sitting by the front door, waiting. "Well, you are ready, I see," Gastrella said, squatting beside him. She took the leash from his mouth and attached it to his collar.

After grabbing a few extra bags, they were out the door, ready for a puppy adventure.

There were two types of dogs in the world. Those that didn't care where they were - if they needed to go they did. Then there were the ones that had a specific spot they preferred to do their business in. Brutus was the latter. A couple days after they moved in, he had picked out his new bathroom, in the park. It was between a five- and-ten-minute walk, depending on their pace, but he always managed to hold it until they arrived.

There was an urgency in the way Brutus tugged her along, especially for an afternoon walk. He normally liked to sniff the fire hydrants. Their pace quickened to a light jog.

In dog sizes, Brutus was somewhere between medium and large. He'd almost tumbled her over on numerous occasions. Walking a dog meant respecting its strength and required her full attention. That was a lesson her brothers still needed to learn.

Knollville Park was split up into sections - a fountain in the middle setting the dividing boundaries. From there, visitors followed one walkway or another to arrive at their preferred destination. For walking a dog, it was preferable to stay as far away from the children's playground as possible. Open grassy areas were the best choice.

Scattered trees became fewer the further in they travelled, giving way to a well-kept field. Over the weekend parts would be utilized for all manners of different sports.

Gastrella used her free hand to wipe her eyes. There was a football game going on and the players were all from her school. Her jaw dropped. Tanner was one of them.

Her heart skipped a beat. She'd found him attractive at school, but seeing him playing in the park without a shirt on was more than she could handle. High school aged boys weren't supposed to be built that well. Every muscle on his body glistened in the sun as he ran. She licked the corner of her mouth, reeling back in the drool attempting to escape. Butterflies fluttered in her stomach as she stood frozen, watching.

A tackle sent several boys tumbling into a pile of testosterone. Chuck offered Tanner a hand up while pointing in Gastrella's direction with his other.

She felt the corner of her lips pulling upwards, the only movement her body wanted to make. She'd never been one to believe in the cliché romance scenes in movies, until that moment.

Tanner's movements slowed to a crawl as he stood, pivoting. She envied the droplets of sweat dribbling down his chest. He flashed his signature sly smile. Even from a distance, their gazes connecting as he raised a hand and waved.

Gastrella felt heat pulsating through her veins. He'd acknowledged her outside school. She bit her bottom lip, willing her own hand to raise and return the gesture. She waved just as a group of girls strutted past.

"As if," Cassidy said, turning around to walk backwards. "He's waving at me, moron." She laughed.

"That's so gross," her friend, Melody, snickered.

Her heart sunk. How could she be so stupid? Of course he wasn't waving at her... she was gross. A wave of heat flushed over her cheeks. Pain ripped through her gut. She needed to leave, but her legs refused to move. Her only hope was to have Brutus pull her out of the park.

"Okay, boy," she said. "Let's go home." She glanced down.

The day couldn't have gotten any worse. This was possibly the humiliation highlight of her life. Shutting her eyes didn't help, the aroma had caught up to her nostrils. The whole time she'd been in crazy stalker mode, Brutus had been leaving a big pile of crap right beside her. He winced, stepping away. Even Brutus knew it was a particularly large and smelly pile of poop.

She pulled out her stash of plastic bags, glad she'd brought more than a few. There was no need for her to worry about crouching down, no one was going to notice if she let one rip with the stench already surrounding her. The handle of Brutus's leash looped around her wrist. This was going to be a two-handed job.

"I hope you are feeling better," she muttered, covering one hand in a plastic bag.

She grabbed a large handful of doggy doo-doo. The fumes alone were enough to bring tears to her eyes. She glanced up, trying to alleviate the stinging sensation. As she gazed directly into the eyes of the enemy, she knew she was in trouble. A bushy tail twitched, mocking her. She could see the squirrel hatching its evil plan. It was a race.

"No!" she screamed, but the squirrel had the jump on her. It ran full speed past Brutus.

Her wrist jolted, causing her to pivot still a squatting position. Barking reached maximum levels. Anyone in the park was sure to have heard Brutus' war cry. The second tug was stronger. She fell backwards, landing on her back on the remains of the poop. The plastic bag flew in the air, emptying its contents all over her.

The squirrel made a safe escape. Brutus turned back. He lay down beside her, covering his eyes with his paws. The barking had been replaced by laughter. Of course, they had seen it all. In that brief moment, she felt all her hopes for a normal school year slip away.

With no dignity left, she stood, scooped up the rest of the poop and made her way to the closest garbage can. Her baseball jersey joined the plastic bags in the garbage. Her tank top underneath was good enough for the walk home.

"Come on, Brutus," she said in a monotone voice.

Brutus whimpered.

"It's okay," she said. "I know it was your arch nemesis. Let's go home."

The pain multiplied threefold during the trek home. After a warm shower and new clothes, she pulled out her favourite hot water bottle. The green terrycloth cover shaped like a frog was well worn from use. Still, it offered her comfort. After filling it, she hopped into bed, pulling the covers over her head. All she wanted was to forget and hope everyone else did too.

Chapter Nine

On weekends, there was no need for an alarm - aromas did the job better than any buzzer could have. The air rewarded her nostrils with the scent of fresh coffee mixed with the tempting sizzle only bacon could create. It was enough bring their whole family to the table.

Saturday was cheat day - the one day of the week Gastrella indulged in all the mouth-watering goodness she missed out on during the week. There was nowhere to go later. It never mattered to her if she let one slip in the privacy of her own room.

She yawned, allowing herself to wake slowly. Her fingers rubbed the sandman's gift from her eyes. There was no need to move any covers, they had been discarded at some point during the night. Cold feet slipped down to the ground, searching out the warmth only fluffy slippers could provide. Her arms lifted up into a full stretch above her head. Changing could wait. The lure of food couldn't.

Gastrella rubbed her midsection as she descended the stairs. It growled a response, having been alerted to the proximity of breakfast. A piece of extra crispy bacon was in her hand before she took a seat. She nibbled on one corner, memories beginning to replace the fogginess of dreamland. Molly's party was in a few hours. If she ate her usual smorgasbord style meal, there was a good chance she'd be farting up a storm that afternoon. The bacon dropped on her plate.

"Is something wrong, dear?" her mother asked.

"I'm going to a friend's house this afternoon," Gastrella explained. "I don't think I should take the chance."

Todd chuckled. "Why?" he asked. "What's a couple farts compared to rolling around in crap? There's no hope for you now."

"What are you talking about?!" Gastrella shrieked. Her brother knew, but how? She hadn't told anyone. She didn't even write it in her diary.

"Yeah," Chuck said, adding his own giggle. "You really are a stinker this time."

Gastrella exchanged glances between her two brothers. "Spill it," she demanded.

"More like drop it," Todd replied. "It's all over the internet. You and Brutus are famous!"

"What's all over the internet?!" Gastrella screeched. The pain in her stomach resurfaced, mounting an assault on her insides.

"That's enough games," Mrs. Balance stated. "What are you two talking about?"

"Here," Chuck offered, holding up his phone. "See for yourself. Gastrella spent the afternoon rolling around in dog crap at the park."

"Where'd you get that?!" Gastrella screamed. "Take it down."

"No can do, sis," Chuck answered, shrugging his shoulders. "I didn't put it up." He stuffed a handful of bacon into his mouth, avoiding answering anything further.

"It wouldn't matter if it came down now, anyways," Todd said. "It's already gone viral. Half the world has seen it."

"Who put it up?" Gastrella asked, sinking back in her chair.

"Some girl named Cassidy," Chuck answered. "She has a ton of followers. This girl is popular."

"Great," Gastrella mumbled. She heading towards the stairs.

"You haven't eaten anything," her mother called after her.

"I'm not hungry," Gastrella replied.

Her door slammed behind her. She flopped on her bed, pulling the covers back over her head and hugging her water bottle. It didn't matter that it was cold now. She longed to go back to the moments before she woke - back to the dream she couldn't remember.

Chapter Ten

Standing outside a front door waiting for it to be answered was one of the worst feelings. The doorbell rang for a second time. Gastrella could feel the weight of stares on her back. The local neighbourhood watch was always ready, willing, and able to catch a would-be criminal in the act, especially in the more upscale areas of Knollville.

Their houses might have been only a few streets apart, but Molly lived in an entirely different world. These homes were three times the size of her own. She glanced in the side window, looking for any signs of movement.

The longer she stood there, the more likely it was that some deranged neighbour would call the local authorities mistaking the birthday present she was holding for a suspicious package. If that happened, a team of firemen were sure to show up and hose her and the parcel down.

It wasn't much, but Gastrella had spent hours looking for the perfect hat. She wasn't an expert, but she was sure friends were supposed to notice little things about each other. If there was one thing she had to pick up on, it was that Molly loved hats.

Her finger twitched, unsure if another ringing was appropriate. Biting her bottom lip, she surveyed the area around her before making one final attempt. The chimes rang louder than a cathedral before Sunday Mass.

"Hey," Molly said, out of breath. "You're early. I wasn't expecting anyone for another half an hour." She opened the door fully, allowing passage in.

Gastrella's eyes widened as she entered the foyer, taking in all of the grandeur it had to offer. A spiral staircase with a balcony at the top, the type she'd only imagined existed, took her breath away. Adding a sophisticated touch, a crystal chandelier hung with pride. It was too high to know for certain if its diamond cut gems were genuine, but it didn't matter. They each glistened as if they were the real deal. A small oval cut window allowed the perfect amount of sun through, reflecting their iridescent shapes on the polished marble floors.

"Everything okay?" Molly asked, taking the outstretched package.

Gastrella pulled her lips back together. "Yeah," she mumbled. She mustered enough courage to move in far enough that the door could close, although her rigid stance remained.

Bells chimed, echoing the sweet songs of birds in love. On this side of the door, it was music to the ears.

"I guess you aren't the only one who is early," Molly said, a shaky chuckle following her words. "You can use my brother's room to change. He's gone for the day. Upstairs and first door on the left. You did bring a suit, right?"

Gastrella nodded, words still unable to form fearing they too weren't good enough to be in the grandiose manor. The railing felt smooth to the touch. Her hand barely kissed its surface as she ascended, a girlish giggle hinging on her breath. Below her other classmates were arriving, each receiving their own instructions as to where to change for the party.

Having two brothers of her own, she was fully prepared to enter a war zone. Her jaw dropped for the second time at the sight of the perfectly pristine condition of Molly's brother's room. Dark browns and blues met in harmony from carpet to curtains to bedding. A desk complete with the latest technology complemented a nook that she might have utilized as extra closet space.

A telescope sat at the window, pointing up to the stars. She laughed. Her solar system was glow-in-the-dark plastic. He, whoever he was, had the real thing to gaze at every night. It suddenly dawned on her, she had only heard Molly mention a brother in passing. Of course, she didn't discuss her own unless absolutely necessary.

Her towel unfolded on the bed, revealing a two piece suit that had never been worn before. It wasn't for a lack of love for the water. She could swim like a fish. It also wasn't because she was ashamed of her body. Bikinis looked good on her. It was all about the anxiety.

Passing gas in public was bad enough. At least in most places she could leave the smell in one place and move to another. Under water, however, things were different. First it was hard not to notice a bunch of bubbles coming up from the wrong end of a person in a pool and second, farts smelt twice as bad when they reached the surface for some reason. She hadn't figured out why and wasn't sure she wanted to know the answer. If she searched it online, it would be in her history forever. Someone seeing that was worse than finding her asking the question *how does one dispose of a dead body*?

She folded her clothes neatly, making sure her underwear and bra were safely wrapped up inside her t-shirt. The door creaked open. Her head popped round the corner, a frown forming when she found she was alone.

"Molly," she said, just slightly louder than a whisper. There was no logic behind her lowered voice, other than the library vibes the upstairs gave her.

There was no answer. She gripped the railing and began her descent, stopping every three stairs to call her friend's name again.

A buzzing roar caught her attention. If there was one noise she knew well, it was that of a blender. Many a morning started out with the natural goodness of a smoothie. She headed in the direction it came from, wondering what concoction Molly was making.

"You should have told me you were making smoothies," she said. "I'm a pro..." Her words faded. Molly wasn't the one standing behind the blender. She gasped.

"Hi," Tanner said, his eyes slanting as he gave her a once-over. "I'd love to hear your recipes sometime. I don't mean to sound pushy, but why, exactly, are you in my house? I don't recall asking for a smoothie making lesson."

"No!" Gastrella exclaimed, gasping. "You didn't. Molly..." She took a step backwards, feeling heat rising in her cheeks. Her breathing exercises weren't going to help in this situation.

"You're friends with Molly," Tanner said, nodding.

Gastrella bit her bottom lip to steady it. "Molly said no one would be home. We were going to have a quick swim."

Tanner's eyebrows arched. "Hence the bikini." He pointed towards her, drink in hand. "It's all starting to make sense now."

"What's starting to make sense?" Cassidy asked, walking in with her entourage. "What is she doing here?"

"She's Molly's friend," Tanner answered. "I thought you were tanning."

"I need some lotion," Cassidy complained. "I was hoping you'd rub some on me. Of course, if you don't want to, Chuck offered."

"Chuck's the man for the job," Tanner replied, staring into his glass of green juice. "I'll be out in a few. I need to talk to my sister."

"I guess I should head back out," Cassidy stated, flipping her hair. "I can smell crap. Can't you?" She glanced at her friends. "I suppose it is hard to get the scent out after rolling around in it." The trio laughed in unison.

Gastrella's arm covered her midsection, feeling the familiar twang caused by building gas. Even the appearance of the lunch table gang didn't alleviate her aching. They were just as scared of being made fun of as she was.

"What's going on?" Molly asked, walking in the room. She placed her hands on her hips, squaring her stance to her brother. "You were going away for the weekend."

"Plans changed," Cassidy snorted. "Nice bathing suit. Mind if we snap a few pictures?" She didn't wait for an answer. "Oh look, it's stretched a bit thin. You can almost see right through it. I guess they stopped making them a few sizes smaller than you need." Laughter echoed through the house.

Time slowed. Gastrella glanced over at her friend. Every breath she took roared through her mind like howling winds. She saw herself reflected in Molly's eyes. It was the sadness that accompanied every mean word that had been uttered in her ear. It was the lack of self-confidence that came with ridicule. It was the blank stare of a victim being bullied over something she had no control over. What was worse than seeing all that in another person's gaze was knowing what came next - the desire for it to stop at any cost. In this case the payment would be made in friendship lost.

Molly's voice shook for only a moment before becoming clear. "This is my party," she said. "Have you met my friends?" She pointed to each of her lunch table mates as she announced their names. There wasn't even a pause before it was over. "And this is Gastrella." The word rolled off her tongue as if it was already beginning the onslaught of mockery.

"Gastrella!" Cassidy laughed. "I have to say, that is the most appropriate name I've ever heard. A stinky name for a girl who rolls in crap."

The standard jokes were hard enough to handle. Knowing it was started by the first person she had ever considered a friend stung. She bolted for the staircase. Her jeans back on, she grabbed her shirt and bag. Her hope for a normal year was the only thing out the door before her. There was no need to look back. It was over. By Monday, everyone and anyone would know her as the gassy girl named Gastrella.

Chapter Eleven

Cassidy and her posse huddled around their usual table, whispering and laughing. Gastrella glanced away, positive they were talking about her or planning some new way to squeeze as much embarrassment as possible from the past weekend's events.

She surveyed the room, her gaze coming to rest on the lunch table that the prior week she had looked forward to sitting at. Even with Molly not there yet, she couldn't bring herself to join them. Her feet shuffled to the exit, carrying her to the one place she belonged: the stairwell.

Although there hadn't been need for recon this year, it was second nature to seek out the least travelled route in the school. The west wing stairs were the perfect place to eat one's lunch... alone.

Paper bag in hand, she slid down to the ground, tossing her backpack to the side. A container popped open, revealing evenly cut stalks of celery. Her cheeks puffed out with releasing air as she glanced down at them. She pushed them aside. That lunch represented everything she had wanted to accomplish and the failure that went along with it. Not letting one rip was only half the battle. She'd stepped up to that task and mastered it, but still ended up with the nickname Stinky Gassy. It was all over social media, written on her locker and even on the blackboards of every class.

She'd come in late to avoid the stares and glares that accompanied low chuckles. It was one thing to have people talk behind her back, it was another when they raised their voices enough to let her know they were doing it.

She pulled out her poetry homework. Her eyes glossed over as she read the words of a joyful teen. A pen scratched them from existence as quickly as the happiness had been removed from her heart. A tear cascaded down her cheek, mingling with the ink on lined paper. She ripped it out of her notebook, crumpling it in a ball. It hit the wall, bouncing down the steps. It was destined for the place where it belonged: the garbage. Her pen wrote a new ode, one more realistic.

A duel begins, dream versus reality.

A gauntlet, etched with hate, strikes the first blow.

The heart weakens, hope is but a coward in the face of cruelty.

The dream retreats, crushed by waves of anticipation.

To be declared a victor one must die.

Society swarms that which is wounded.

The hands of a once friend strikes the final blow.

In reality we are alone and alone is where we shall remain.

There is no place safe for nature's freak.

Only the strong survive.

The book slammed closed at the sound of the bell. It was time for another bout to begin. Her gloves were laced, but she wasn't sure she had enough left in the tank to defend herself, let alone throw a punch. Life was easier if she accepted her place and stayed in it. That was exactly what she intended to do.

Chapter Twelve

The blackboard was empty. The professor had either been in there early or erased any messages before she walked in. That was something, at least. Maybe there was at least one class she could make it through without feeling sick. She sighed, realizing she was allowing a tiny spark of hope back in. That was a mistake she knew she'd pay for sooner or later.

"Take your seats," Mr. Jenkins ordered. "I hope everyone completed their homework because we are having a surprise test today."

Gastrella kept her eyes on the ground, taking her usual place. This was her first class with Tanner since the unfortunate incident. Making her way through hallways of gawkers was nothing compared to having to look in Tanner's eyes. His judgment was too much to handle.

Mr. Jenkins placed a test on her desk. Pure white stared up at her, the questions hidden until all papers had been distributed. Of all the forms of evaluation at her teacher's disposal, this was the easiest. Writing answers was as solitary as possible - head down, no talking. That meant there would be no sly comments or condescending glares.

A glimmer of sadness attached itself to her pencil case, born from the memory of how nice Tanner had been that first day. Still, she needed to find her lucky pencil to write with. She cringed at the thought of the noise the zipper would make, pulling as gently as possible. Inside, she pushed around various writing instruments, looking for the ugliest.

It had been cheap looking when her father gifted it to her years ago to ease the strain of exams. Ever since, tests were the only thing she used it for. She flipped it over in her hand, examining every bite mark she'd made. Pink unicorns and rainbows on the shaft were still identifiable, although somewhat warped. The eraser that had once sat perched on the end had disappeared, but the other side still did its job. One finger pressed against the lead tip. It was sharp enough to make it through today. One pencil, one eraser and one white piece of paper was all that remained on her desk. She was ready.

Mr. Jenkins glanced at the clock on the wall and then at his wrist watch. "You have until the end of class to finish." He paused, eyes locked on the second hand ticking away. "You can begin... now." Taking a seat at his desk, he pulled out a newspaper to whittle away the time.

Gastrella flipped over her paper, taking a moment to scan through the questions. They were all standard equations, with nothing too easy or too hard. For her, this was a walk in the park. There was no question she could ace every part with ease. If she had been asked to solve a question on the blackboard, or explain her answers verbally, she would have been in trouble. One nervous moment always led to another and, before she knew it, a buildup of gas that refused to wait to be set free. She placed her name at the top of the page, readying herself to tackle the first problem.

Silence lingered in the air, nothing more than a suspended moment before disaster struck. Hushed everyday chatter left behind a gaping void begging to be filled. Gastrella had been in quiet rooms before, but not like this. A complete lack of noise terrified her. Those sounds that normally passed unnoticed had nowhere to hide. The scratching of lead on paper behind her was proof of that. Whoever was causing it, was pressing too hard. A snap confirmed her thoughts.

Using the forms of meditation she'd learnt, she breathed in and out, trying to remain as quiet as possible. The sound of her own breath echoed tenfold in her mind as she tackled the next question, resisting the urge to glance at the rest of the class.

The next noise, however, was even more disturbing. She had heard it tens of thousands of times in her life and knew exactly what it meant - a stomach ache. This time the grumbling noise didn't come from her, though. Someone else in the room had gas.

She chomped on her pencil, not from contemplating an answer, but from fear. Things she couldn't control always turned out bad for her. Walking any tightrope meant that at any second, someone else could push her over one side or the other. Right now, her name was only mentioned in whispers behind her back. Even with it written on her locker and a few blackboards, things could have been much worse. One stink bomb, hers or not, had the potential to cause the whole school to ridicule her to her face. Whoever said words can never hurt was wrong.

Another gurgle left a cold sweat on her brow. The numbers on the paper before her blurred. She needed to escape - run away. If she wasn't in the room, she couldn't be blamed. There was no exit, though. No teacher allowed a student to go to the bathroom during a test and she was nowhere near finished. Pain radiated in her midsection, the building anxiety bring to life her worst fears. She breathed through each wave, begging any god who would listen to help her through the next half hour.

"Holy crap," Chuck blurted out.

"Is there a problem?" Mr. Jenkins asked.

"Yeah," Chuck answered. "Someone let one rip and it stinks. Can we open a window or something?" He waved a hand in front of his face.

Gastrella bit her bottom lip. A silent but deadly was the worst possible fart for someone to let loose. With no audible noise, the blame could easily be shifted to her and she knew it would be.

"O-M-G," another student yelled. "That's rotten."

"Mr. Jenkins," Tanner started, "I can't work under these circumstances. The smell is making me ill. Can I go to the nurse?"

Laughter erupted through the classroom.

"You may not," the teacher answered, heading down the aisle. He stopped about halfway to the back. "Chuck, open a window."

Another putrid blast filled the air, choking those it came in contact with. Tanner coughed, covering his nose with his arm. Chuck stood to move to the window, falling to the ground in theatrics instead.

"I... can't... make... it," he groaned. "Need... air."

Gastrella made one mistake, turning around. The laughter had been too much for her not to sneak a peek. Her eyes made contact with Chuck's. The world slowed to a crawl as the boy extended a finger in her direction. Life flashed before her eyes. A new worst moment ever was emerging. There was no way to stop what had already been set in motion.

"She did it!" Chuck bellowed. "Gastrella the Gassy!"

That was the end of everything she'd striven for. In one split second, her world had reverted to exactly where she was before coming to Knollville. Forevermore she was going to have the nicknames Gassy or Stinky. Most of the time when people make fun of others, they got bored or find something worse to tease someone else about. These was nothing worse than a girl who farts a lot with gas in her name. She was doomed.

Laughter might have covered up the rumblings in her tummy, but with every giggle and snicker, the pain increased. She was a volcano building towards an eruption. No matter how hard she squeezed her buttocks together, something was bound to squeak out.

"Hey, Tanner," Chuck called out. "She left her undies in your room on the weekend. Do they smell that bad?"

Gastrella felt the colour draining for her face. Her thoughts traced her steps at Tanner's house. Her underwear were wrapped in her clothes on his bed from when she changed. She must have dropped them in the rush to escape. How could she have not noticed?

The laughter turned to a chorus of gasps. She was not only stinky, but the class whore as well. That was a step in the wrong direction.

The stinging in her eyes matched the aches in her midsection. She needed to escape before both exploded, making the situation even worse. She grabbed her backpack and bolted for the door, already knowing from experience it didn't matter what she said, no one was going to believe her.

Chapter Thirteen

"What did you say that for?" Tanner complained, pushing Chuck against a locker after class. "You know she ran out of my place in a hurry and left her underwear by mistake."

"What's the big deal?" Chuck asked, pushing back. "If I didn't know better, I'd think you had a thing for her." He snorted, heading to their next class. "That girl is a social nightmare."

Tanner brushed the hair from his face. His fist made contact with a locker. Letting it slip that he had to return undies to Gastrella had been a huge mistake. He'd known it as soon as the words passed through his lips. Chuck might have been his best friend, but when it came to being a jerk, he won the award every time. The empty hall meant it was time for the last class of the day.

The room fell silent as he entered, with every gaze locked on his movements. Being a team player, he was used to the limelight. This feeling, however, was entirely different. He was being scrutinized in every way, leaving him feeling both violated and vulnerable.

Cassidy's hips swung as she strutted across the room. "Please tell me it isn't true," she said, chuckling. One hand covered her mouth.

"What isn't true?" Tanner asked, glancing over her shoulder at Chuck. He tossed his back pack on the floor beside his desk before taking a seat, oblivious to the chatter around him.

"You and the stinky girl," Cassidy snickered. "I hear you have her underwear in your bag. Is it true?"

Tanner shook his head, shooting daggers from his gaze towards Chuck. "It's not what you think," he started. Before he could finish, Cassidy snatched his bag and was rummaging through. "Hey!"

"O-M-G!" Cassidy exclaimed, holding up a pink pair of panties with little hearts printed all over. She twirled them over her head.

"Give them back!" Tanner ordered, chasing her around the room. He caught her in one corner as the teacher closed the door.

"Take your seats!"

"Gladly," Tanner replied, shoving the undies in his pocket. "For the record, nothing happened. They were left by mistake from a pool party my sister had. I was merely returning them."

"Right," Cassidy replied, rolling her eyes.

"You were there," Tanner argued. "You know she left in a hurry."

"Yeah," Cassidy agreed. "Come to think of it, I was there." A mischievous smile graced her lips. "I think I took a few pictures that day, too."

"Good," Tanner said, returning to his desk. "Then we can drop this, right? Promise me you will leave Gastrella alone."

Cassidy licked her bottom lip, glossing it better than any lipstick could have. "Okay, I won't bother Gastrella, just for you."

"Thank you," Tanner replied.

"If we could," the teacher complained, "sometime today, I'd like to start this class. I am sure whatever fascinating topic you two are discussing can wait until after school." He turned his back to write on the blackboard.

A series of buzzes sounded, half the class pulling out their phones. Tanner glanced from side to side as a series of stifled giggles erupted among his peers. His own cell vibrated. He glanced down at a picture of his sister from the weekend. He had forgotten how her swimsuit had been a little too tight and ripped a bit at the back. Cassidy had preserved the moment forever. It wouldn't take long before it circulated through the entire school. He shook his head, glancing in Cassidy's direction.

Cassidy shrugged her shoulders. "I said I'd leave Gastrella alone. I never said anything about Molly. You really should talk to her about finding things that actually fit her."

"You two!" the teacher bellowed. "Move your desks to opposite sides of the room. One more interruption and you'll find yourselves in the office."

Tanner glanced out the window in time to see Gastrella jogging down the sidewalk. At least the pressure was off her for the moment. Now all he had to worry about was his sister.

He needed to reach her after school before news of the leaked picture did.

Chapter Fourteen

Faking being sick was an easy task. Having spent most of her life avoiding being made fun of meant it was second nature to her. In Knollville it was even easier. Her whole family knew how well things had been going for her since they arrived. There was no reason for anyone to doubt she had come down with the flu.

If there was one thing that stood true ninety nine percent of the time, it was that parents were always technologically challenged. The speed at which things advanced in the world left previous generations in the dust. Her family was no different. Instead of picking up a digital thermometer that went in her ear, she was opening her mouth as a glass one slid under her tongue.

"Keep it still," her mother ordered. "We want a proper reading."

That was easy to say, but not quite as easy to do. The thermometer poked the underside of her tongue, making her cringe. She already knew what the results were going to be, between a hundred and one and a hundred and two. That was the optimal fever, being too high to leave the house and too low to warrant a trip to the doctor. It was also easy to replicate. First she used her hot water bottle to warm her forehead and cheeks. Passing the mother's touch phase was a vital stage in the plan. Then, while her mother fetched her first aid kit, Gastrella drank hot water from the tap, warming the inside of her mouth. It didn't taste good, but did the job where it counted.

Her mother sighed. "You'll have to stay in bed," she stated, holding out her hand. "You know the rules. I'll need all devices."

Being sick in the Balance household meant doing exactly that and nothing else. Gastrella handed over her remote controls, laptop and phone. Any normal teenager would have taken issue with the loss. To her, however, it was a blessing. There wasn't an ounce of desire to log onto any form of social media and see how bad the situation at school actually was.

People were twice as cruel when hidden safely behind a keyboard.

A handful of clothespins and an assortment of old sheets snapped into place, creating the shell of a tent over her bed. After that it was all about the decor. High peaks were a must, allowing for easy movement while inside. No fort was complete without pillows lining every closed side. That wasn't just for comfort. They acted as a hiding spot for all her needs, including books, a flashlight and snacks. They also left a middle section empty - perfect to fill with quilts and throws. Once everything was set up, she was ready to become a blanket burrito and hide from all that was wrong in her life.

The following days were as uneventful as possible. She remained in her fort, leaving only to use the bathroom or wash. All that passed were days. Every feeling remained the same. Staying bundled up only served to put off the inevitable. At some point, she would have to face the world again.

There was only so long a person could fake an illness before someone either caught on or started insisting on a trip to the emergency room. Neither of which were appealing. The thought of needles poking her tiny veins to find out nothing was wrong sent shivers up and down her spine screaming *no*.

She had reached her max and knew it. Ten was the optimal number of days to get over cold or flu. It was time to step out of her cocoon and face the music, or in her case, snickers. The tent was down and she was dressed before her mother walked in, thermometer in hand.

"Oh, thank goodness," Mrs. Balance said, covering her chest with one hand. "I was worried that bug had a hold of you. I was ready to make an appointment with the doctor for this afternoon."

"I feel much better, Mom," Gastrella replied. "I need to get back to school. I don't want to miss too much."

"You know," Mrs. Balance said, "if you ever need to talk about something, your father and I are always here for you." She held out her daughter's phone. "Try to have a good day."

"I will," Gastrella answered, wondering if she had actually fooled anyone at all. "Mom... thanks."

Her mother nodded, closing the door behind her.

Chapter Fifteen

Gastrella inched forward in the line, waiting to pay for a single bottle of water. Being out of routine for any amount of time longer than three days usually meant something was forgotten. In her case, it was lunch. She let out a huff, scanning the cafeteria from her place in the queue. Not much had changed. Most of the same groups were intact. A swift glance was all she allowed herself of the popular table. Although it was business as usual there, Tanner was noticeably absent. Likewise, his sister also hadn't taken her place with the group of misfits. She tossed her bottle in the air, catching it on the way back down. A quiet stairwell was waiting for her.

"Hey."

Gastrella jumped, feeling a tug on her arm before hearing the word. "Oh, hey," she replied.

"Where you been?" Abigail asked in her usual monotone voice.

"I... I," Gastrella stuttered, "was sick."

"You coming to sit down?" Abigail arched an eyebrow, waiting for a reply.

Gastrella shook her head. "Molly," she grimaced. "We haven't spoken since her party."

"Well, she isn't here," Abigail stated, heading towards the awkward table. She took her usual seat without a word spoken to the others already gathered.

Gastrella's inner voice screamed for her to flee, but instead she followed. Companionship was a basic human need. That trumped worrying about the invitation being a trap that would end in another social media scandal. She took a seat, glancing from one person to another. No one said a word. The silence grew louder than the calamity of voices from other tables.

"So," she said, her eyes flickering wider, "where is Molly?" If she thought the silence had been unnerving before, it was twice as bad after that question.

"Were you cut off from civilization?" Abigail asked.

"No," Gastrella lied. "Well, maybe. My parents have a rule... anyone who is sick isn't allowed to use the internet."

"Weird rule," Abigail replied, rolling her eyes. "Molly is in the hospital. She has been for a couple of days."

"Hospital!" Gastrella shrieked. "What for?"

"She tried to kill herself," Mitsy answered in as loud a voice as Gastrella had ever heard her use. "It's been big news."

"What?!" Gastrella exclaimed. "I didn't see that coming."

"No one did," Lief stated. "It was all sorts of nastiness. After you took-off from the party, the rest of us went out to the pool. Tanner and Molly argued over who had the right to use it and they ended up agreeing we'd all share. Someone took pictures of Molly in her swimsuit."

"Even worse," Mitsy said in a voice only slightly louder than a whisper. "At one point, it ripped. None of us noticed at the time."

"Whoever took the pictures sent them out by text," Lief explained. "It took a couple days, but it circulated back to her."

"She was pretty devastated," Abigail said, focusing on her charcoal sketching. "Then it went from bad to worse. Somehow, the picture landed on the front page of the school newspaper and stuffed as flyers were additional poses. People were laughing and calling her names."

"It was the underwear incident that did it, though," Mitsy said.

"Underwear?" Gastrella mumbled, remembering her own issue with that very subject.

"Someone bought a pair of huge underwear and wrote her name across the front of them before hanging them over the cafeteria doors on Friday," Abigail explained. "They were big enough to cover the top of both doors. I didn't know they made them that big."

"That's terrible," Gastrella replied. "The people responsible are being punished, I hope." All gazes lifted to meet hers.

"There is no proof of who was to blame," Lief explained. "We all know who was behind it." He glanced over at Cassidy. "But they won't dole out punishment without definitive proof."

"Can't they check phone records?" Gastrella asked.

"Apparently it was a non-traceable number," Lief answered. "It's becoming more common now that there are stricter punishments for bullying."

"Great," Gastrella muttered. "I thought laws would make the situation better."

"They never do," Abigail retorted. "They only end up making smarter criminals." She rolled her eyes. "Where there's a will, there's a way. In high school, there is always a will."

"I thought I was next up for slaughter," Gastrella groaned. "I was sure I was going to be eaten alive when I returned."

"Why?" Abigail asked.

"There was a situation in math class," Gastrella replied. "I figured it would have gone viral by now."

"Oh," Tim said, wagging a finger in her direction. "You mean Tanner having your underwear in his backpack."

"Good to see it wasn't totally forgotten," Gastrella grimaced.

"Yeah, we only know because Tanner told everyone the truth," Tim explained. "He got into it with Cassidy in the next class... announced to everyone that nothing happened."

"He did that?" Gastrella questioned.

"Yeah," Abigail said. "Weird, huh. I didn't take him as the type to stick his neck out on the line."

"How is Molly?" Gastrella asked, fidgeting with the label on her water bottle. "I mean, she's going to be alright, isn't she?"

The charcoal in Abigail's hand pressed hard against her sketch pad, darkening out the picture she had taken weeks to create. "She's in rough shape. They don't know if she'll pull through. Her odds aren't good, from what I understand."

Gastrella glanced over her shoulder at Cassidy laughing in the centre of a group of boys. If she was to blame, she wasn't showing an ounce of remorse. Her gaze spanned left, coming to settle on another group. They were known as the resident witches of Knollville High. With what she'd just heard about Molly's condition, perhaps a little witchcraft might help. At the very least, it couldn't hurt.

Chapter Sixteen

Penelope glanced up from her lunch, her gaze meeting that of a stranger. It wasn't often people outside their clique stopped by their lunch table for a friendly chat. Normally, one of them would snarl or hiss. That was enough to send most teens scampering away in fear. This girl, however, held some interest. She was an enigma. Nobody knew much about her other than a few whispers. Even her name had remained a secret for the first week of school. Still, somehow, she'd managed to find a way to make one of the most popular boys in school stick up for her. That alone deserved credit.

"What?" Madison snapped, her tongue peeking out the side of blackened lips. "Don't just stare."

"I'm..."

"Gastrella," Penelope answered. "We know who you are. What we don't know is why you are here... standing in front of us."

"May I?" Gastrella asked, motioning towards an empty chair.

Madison kicked it out from under the table. "Go ahead. You have our curiosity." Her nostrils flared, accentuating a silver piercing.

"I heard you were..."

"Witches?" Madison cackled. "We don't turn people into frogs or make love potions, so you can parade Tanner around on your arm."

"No!" Gastrella exclaimed, waving her arms in front of her. "I didn't think you could. I mean, I don't actually know what you can do."

"So what is it we can do for you?" Penelope asked, clicking her black fingernails together to make an unnerving noise.

"It's about Molly," Gastrella explained.

"The girl who tried to kill herself?" Flora asked in a soft tone that matched her pastel-like appearance. Everything about the girl was soothing, from her voice, to her appearance and even the light floral scent that accompanied her every move. Her faded pink dress had layers that flowed even in the absence of a breeze.

"Yes," Gastrella replied. "She isn't doing well. I thought maybe you could..."

"Heal her?" Madison asked, arching pencilled in eyebrows. "We aren't doctors."

"I know," Gastrella blurted out. "I didn't mean to offend. I don't know a lot about Wicca, but I have heard of ways to heal the spirit. I thought it might help. I'm sorry to bother you."

Penelope alternated her glances between the girl walking away and Cassidy grinding her body as close to as many members of the football team as she could without being sent to the office for inappropriate behaviour. "Huh," she grunted, shaking her head.

"Oh no," Madison said, a finger waving in the air, the nail pierced with a miniature charm of a wand. "I know that look. We are not taking on Cassidy and the entire senior class."

"A girl is in the hospital fighting for her life," Penelope argued. "We should do something to rectify the situation."

"I'll order the flowers," Flora suggested. "That's the best we can do to help her other than sending her positive vibes."

"But why should Cassidy get away with it?" Penelope questioned. "Technically, it is attempted murder in my books."

"We aren't judge, jury, or executioner," Madison complained. "Besides, are you sure it isn't her newfound interest in Scott that has your feathers ruffled?"

"Everything about her ruffles my feathers." Penelope crossed her arms over her chest. "She deserves a taste of her own medicine."

"I don't know what you are planning," Madison said, "but we aren't going to break any rules. I'm already on probation for unnecessary magic use. I meant what I said... no love potions."

"I'll make sure we don't do anything illegal," Penelope agreed. "With a little research, I'm sure we can come up with something to teach Cassidy a lesson or two."

"I don't have any flowers for that," Flora said, a frown crossing tiny lips. "I won't be much help."

"That's okay," Penelope said, chuckling. "Let's concentrate with getting Molly better first. I have a feeling she will need several bouquets. We have an entire year to deal with Miss Popularity after that."

"Do you still have a contact at the hospital?" Madison questioned. "We'll be blowing smoke up a closed chimney if we can't get them delivered."

"I still know a person or two who are happy to aid where practical medicine fails," Flora admitted. "How should I address the cards?"

"With our names, of course," Madison snorted. "We deserve some credit for being good little witches once in a while."

"Done!" Flora said, clapping her hands together. "The flowers will start arriving this evening."

The bell rang.

Chapter Seventeen

Tanner watched the young woman wearing a pink and white striped dress as she glided across the room with a large bouquet of brightly coloured daisies in her hand. Until the moment she set them down on the stand beside his sister's bed, he hadn't noticed the clear vase they were sitting in. The floral scents reached his nostrils within seconds. He turned to thank the woman, but found his voice was lost.

A chill accompanied the meek smile her otherwise solemn pale face offered. Goosebumps on his arm screamed warnings of all things unnatural. The woman extended an envelope in his direction. His hand moved, as if commanded to accept the offering.

Tanner glanced down at one word, *Molly*, written in an old-fashioned form of calligraphy. A wax seal was placed on the back, ensuring only intended eyes would read the contents.

By the time he looked up, the woman was gone. Not a word had been uttered or a noise sounded. Both the chill and goosebumps retreated along with her. His eyes eagerly searched the corners of the room, already knowing they would find nothing.

Without wasting any time, he ripped open the envelope and read the contents.

Flowers of colour so very bright

Help heal Molly's pain on this very night

May calming scents warm to her core

So she may join us in life once more

Penelope, Madison & Flora

He glanced over at the flowers, then at his sister. He rubbed his eyes, watching as a small amount of colour returned to her face. Within the hour, the flowers wilted. As if on cue, the young woman returned with a bunch of lavender flowers to replace those that had withered.

Tanner shifted in his seat before accepting the next envelope.

Into these flowers release your pain

Do not take these gifts in vain

Take their strength and hold it dear

Release negativity, hate and fear

Madison, Flora & Penelope

Thoughts ran through Tanner's mind. Who was this mysterious delivery woman? Did she work for the hospital? Why couldn't he ask her? He glanced up, already knowing she had vanished.

Over the course of the next hour, he watched the flowers shrivel up and die. Someone had hit the fast forward button on their existence. At the same time, his sister looked healthier... stronger.

He closed his eyes only for a split-second. When they opened, he almost jumped out of his skin at the sight of the woman standing before him, another envelope held out. He glanced at a bunch of pink roses that had replaced those that had expired.

He accepted both the envelope and the fact that his voice had retreated once again, offering the woman a nod of gratitude. She returned a nod of her own, before disappearing. Tanner shook his head. His eyes hadn't left the woman, yet he had no recollection of how she exited the room. She was simply gone.

He broke the third seal with an audible crack. Molly's fingers twitched. Tanner pulled out the note and unfolded it, his hands shaking.

We call out to a friend

May these roses your spirit mend

When day doth break from night

Trust us Molly you'll be alright.

Flora, Penelope & Madison

Tanner opened the curtains and watched as darkness faded. For the first time, he noticed the similarities between the rising sun and an opening gold-trimmed, orange flower.

He held out his hand, allowing the amber glow to pour through his fingers. He felt the warmth and healing of the early morning rays as they inched closer and closer to his sister's body. At first contact, Molly's lungs filled to capacity. He raced for the button, summoning a nurse.

A middle-aged woman strolled in. "Is everything okay?"

"My sister!" Tanner exclaimed. "She moved."

The nurse rushed to Molly's bedside. After checking her pulse, she smiled. "She seems stronger. The doctor will be by soon. Were you here all night? You should go home and get some sleep."

"I don't want her to be alone," Tanner replied. "I'd like to be here when she wakes up."

"She's stronger, but she isn't out of the woods yet," the nurse stated. "You go home and get some rest. We'll call you if there is any change."

Tanner nodded. "Oh," he called after her. "The nurse who was here last night, I'd like to thank her."

"I was the only one on duty last night," the nurse replied. "There was no one else here."

"She came in three times... delivering flowers," Tanner argued. He nodded to the empty table beside the bed.

The nurse glanced over and back at him. "There are no flowers. You probably fell asleep and dreamt the whole thing. It happens more often than you might imagine in hospitals."

"I swear she was here," Tanner complained. "She was wearing a pink and white striped dress."

The nurse laughed. "A candy stripper... this hospital hasn't used volunteers like that in years. Trust me, you'll feel better after a few hours' sleep."

Tanner watched her leave before checking around and under the night stand. He even looked through the garbage with no luck. Had he imagined the whole thing?

Rubbing his eyes with the palms of his hands, he conceded he was over tired. With slightly parted lips, a yawn escaped. He reached in his pocket for enough change for a coffee, but pulled out the three notes instead.

Chapter Eighteen

Gastrella tugged on the leash, hoping Brutus was done sniffing whatever another animal left to be smelt. The best part of walking a dog was the actual physical activity. Standing still on a corner seemed counter-productive. At least in the park, there was a view.

She let one rip, cursing herself for wearing tight pants all day. That was the worst for causing cramps. Brutus glanced up at her and whined.

"Oh, like you don't do it," she complained. "Remember the squirrel incident. I didn't judge you for that."

A single *woof* was her answer. Brutus pulled her forward as another bout of gas finished brewing. A family of ducks could have been following them with all the quacking noises bringing up the rear. Even Brutus did a double take, checking behind them.

Gastrella chuckled. With no one around, she could accept how funny her own farting actually could be. It was only when other people laughed at her she had a problem. Her thoughts drifted to Molly. They were similar in so many ways. Suicide had been on her to-do list the previous year, but news of the move had stopped those plans from being put into motion.

Everyone knew that suicide happened, especially among teens who were picked on in school. So why did students still harass each other? Why were people given labels? Why did they have to sit at different tables? Why couldn't a person be accepted for just what they were... an individual?

The emptiness of the park aided her deep thought. She wasn't completely without fault. All those years she suffered, she had thought of herself as the only victim. That simply wasn't true. There were so many others... Molly, Abigail, Lief, Tim, even the trio of Knollville witches were unjustly stereotyped. She hadn't reached out to anyone, fearing what would happen. A handful of people she didn't even know had been running her life.

A squirrel ran past. Brutus took offence to its insolence. Muscles tensed in all four limbs as he hurtled after his arch nemesis. His pink tongue hung out one side of his open mouth, drool flying backwards as he picked up speed. The leash ripped from her hand before she could adjust her grip. She screamed, giving chase, but was no match for his speed. Within seconds, neither Brutus nor the squirrel were anywhere to be found.

Gastrella slouched on a park bench, defeated. This was another thing to add to her list of growing failures. All she could do was hope Brutus was smart enough to return to his favourite spot after his prey escaped. Her head hung low, gaze fixed on the red mark the leash had left on the palm of her hand. It stung, almost as much as her eyes. A wet nose nudged her hand.

"Brutus." she exclaimed, rubbing behind both of his ears. A pair of shoes caught her attention. She glanced up into warm brown eyes.

"Hey," Tanner said, taking a seat beside her. "I figured he might have been lost." He handed her the leash.

"Thank you," she croaked, her mouth becoming dry. That was the least of her problems, though. She needed to keep her eyes focused on her pet, not wanting to stare long enough for her crush to be noticed.

An uneasy tension grew between them, fed by the lingering silence. He wasn't leaving. For her to make the first move after he rescued Brutus was rude. She was stuck waiting for him to say goodbye first.

"How's Molly?" she blurted out.

He side-eyed her, the corners of his lips turning up ever so slightly. "Actually," he replied, "she woke up last night. She should be home by the end of the week."

"That's great!" Gastrella exclaimed.

"She still has a long way to go," he continued. "There will be a slew of doctors appointments and therapy in her future. She could use a friend."

"I'm not sure I'm..."

"You mean more to her than you know," Tanner interrupted. "She felt bad for what happened at her party. It would mean a lot if you forgave her."

"I understand why," Gastrella admitted. "Maybe you can let her know that. I've been there. When she feels better, we can talk."

"I'll pass it on," Tanner said.

"Thank you," Gastrella offered. "Not just for playing messenger. I heard you told everyone the truth about me."

A chuckle escaped his lips with all the warmth of a roaring fire. "I owed you that," he replied. "I probably shouldn't have brought your panties to school. I wanted to return them."

Gastrella pursed her lips together, A red tinge taking over her pale face. "Awkward," she said, her eyebrows arching. Her gaze locked on the leash held tightly in both hands. Brutus lay down and covered his eyes, letting out a high-pitched whine.

This time, Tanner's laughter exploded. The damn had been breached and every bit came pouring out. He bit his lip, taking control once again, but it wouldn't last. A snort set off another series of giggles. He covered his mouth, sealing the exit momentarily. That wasn't the only place happiness comes from, though. The more he bottled it up, the move it overflowed from his eyes.

Tanner breathed in deeply. "I can drop them off at your house, if you want. Maybe later tonight?"

"Awkward!" Gastrella exclaimed. "I suppose you want to explain to my dad why you have my underwear, too."

His lips trembled, threatening to release more emotions. "Sorry," he said. "I didn't think of that. I don't think I should bring them back to school..."

"No!" Gastrella blurted out. This time she snorted. "I think enough people have already seen them."

"They are cute," Tanner retorted, earning him a punch in the arm. "Hey. I was only telling the truth."

"Awkward!" she exclaimed, but it wasn't. If anything, the tension between them had been relieved. "You could burn them. I don't think I could ever bring myself to wear them again anyways."

"Okay," Tanner said, standing. He wiped the palms of his hands on his jeans. "Burn them it is. I'll see you at school."

"Yup," Gastrella replied. "Oh, Tanner... thank you again for everything." She held up her end of the leash. "Come on, Brutus. Let's go home."

Chapter Nineteen

"Quiet down!" Mr. LeStat bellowed from the stage.

Gordon LeStat had been the principle of Knollville High for as many years as anyone could remember. In fact, he came from a long line of headmasters. Streaks of grey peppered his dark hair. A full three-piece suit kept any other indicators of age hidden from view. He was a remarkably well kept man who managed to remain mysteriously unnoticeable. Even the annual staff photographs that lined the walls of his prestigious school lacked any resemblances of his image.

"Settle into your seats." His voice rose without the need for a microphone. Not even the boom of thunder directly overhead could compete with the reach of his tone.

The students complied with his request. Within moments, the pinging pitter-patter of raindrops on the roof was all that could be heard. A storm was upon them. The lights flickered, threatening darkness.

Gastrella shifted her position. The plastic seats that had been set up in rows were anything but comfortable. She was already regretting her chosen spot at the back of the room. Glancing over hundreds of heads, she couldn't make out the features of anyone she knew.

"Don't worry, the school has back-up generators," LeStat announced. "I am sure you are all aware of the reason why you have been called into an assembly. If you don't have a clue, I'll tell you. We are here to discuss bullying. We here at Knollville High have a no-tolerance policy, which we have always prided ourselves on. It's disturbing to find out that something slipped through right under our noses."

Thunder cracked twice as loud, eliciting a series of gasps and grumbles from the gathered students. The lights flickered, extinguishing for a moment before buzzing back on - the generator taking over for the lost power source. Gastrella jumped, startled to find the previously empty seat beside her occupied.

"Sorry," Tanner whispered. "I saw you sitting here and thought we could both use a friendly face close by."

"As I was saying," LeStat continued, "certain pictures have been circulating around the school and on social media sites. There was also an incident involving the cafeteria doors. These activities are being investigated and the culprits, once found, will be dealing with not only myself and the school board, but the police as well."

A wave of mumbles erupted, growing in strength as each second passed. Tanner nodded towards Cassidy hanging off Chuck's arm, a coy smile plastered on her face. "Looks like they aren't too worried about any of this."

"If anyone has any information, they can see myself or any teacher to discuss what they know in private," LeStat suggested. "Until then, to handle the issues that have arisen, we have two new members of the staff. Mrs. Mindki will be helping students deal with issues of bullying and Ms. Natty will be holding group sessions dealing with alleviating anxiety and depression within our student body. I urge you all to take advantage of their knowledge and expertise. Before I turn the stage over to them, I'd like to take a moment to mention the victim of this cruel bout of attacks."

"Are you going to tell Mr. LeStat?" Gastrella asked.

Tanner sighed. "I can't prove anything. There is nothing to link them to the events. They covered their trail."

"As you may have heard," LeStat continued, "the young girl in question attempted to take her own life." He waited for the grumbles to peter out. "We were lucky this time. She is going to make a full recovery. Next time, however, things may not turn out as well... someone could die. That's something each of us should think about."

"Oh," Tanner said, reaching into his backpack. "I have something..."

"Not here!" Gastrella exclaimed, garnering her a few odd stares. "I told you to burn them."

Tanner chuckled. "Not that," he replied. "These." He pulled out the notes from the flowers. "Do you know why Penelope and friends sent flowers to the hospital?"

"They did?" Gastrella asked, her face lighting up.

"Yeah," Tanner replied. "I think they had something to do with her recovery, but I don't know why."

"I asked them to," Gastrella explained.

"You asked witches to help my sister?" Tanner questioned, one eyebrow arching. "What possessed you to do that?"

"I don't know," Gastrella admitted. "I guess I figured at the very least, it couldn't hurt any. I saw them at lunch and had this weird feeling I needed to talk to them... so I did."

Tanner shook his head, his smile widening. "I think they are the reason she pulled through."

"Sh," Mr. Jenkins said, pulling up a chair behind them. "I would have thought you'd want to hear what was going on."

"Sorry, sir," Tanner replied.

"We won't be asking you to sign up for the group sessions," Mrs. Natty stated. "Instead, we will post the time and location of our meetings and all students are welcome to attend. I want each of you to know there is no problem too small or too large to tackle. These bi-weekly meetings are aimed at supporting each of you as you try to make sense of whatever you may be going through. I realize not everyone will attend, but the door is open if you feel the need."

"What if we all do show up?" A student yelled out, followed by a wave of giggles.

"Then we'll have to find a suitable place for everyone," Mrs. Natty replied. "If we have to make several extra meetings, that's what we'll do. The goal is to make sure no one feels as if they are alone. If there are any questions, feel free to approach me anytime. I am here for you." She stepped back.

"Thank you, Mrs. Natty," LeStat said. "Please return to your classes in an orderly fashion."

Chapter Twenty

Gastrella peeked through the small rectangular window on the door before opening it. She'd fought with herself for days over whether or not to attend Mrs. Natty's first meeting. Anxiety had plagued her for as long as she could remember; sharing that with someone other than her doctor, however, seemed strange.

The classroom had been rearranged, pushing desks to the side and forming a circle out of chairs. If there were a table in the middle it could have been lunch. With the exception of Mrs. Natty, the only others there were Tim, Lief, Misty and Abigail. She inhaled deeply, taking a seat beside her peers.

They had more in common than she originally thought. The strange part was if Mrs. Natty hadn't called a meeting, she never would have known each of them suffered from anxiety and depression as well. As each day passed, she was learning she wasn't as alone as she had thought.

"I take it you all are acquainted," Mrs. Natty said, glancing at each of them and receiving nods in return. "Well then, let's get started..."

"Shouldn't we wait for a few others to arrive?" Lief asked.

"There aren't going to be any others," Abigail replied. "We're still the biggest losers in the school." She rolled her eyes.

"You aren't losers," Mrs. Natty said. "Having a social disorder is more common than you know. This group will grow as time passes." She locked eyes on the Abigail's sketch book. "Would anyone like to introduce themselves and tell us a bit about why you are here?"

"I would," Tanner said from the door. He shut it behind him. "I'm Tanner and I have an anxiety problem."

"Right," Abigail huffed.

"I know it's hard to believe," Tanner said, licking his lips. "I am on the football team and socially I don't have a problem. It's tests I can't handle. My stomach gets tied in knots and I clam up."

Gastrella gasped, her eyes widening. "It was you that day." She stood, squaring her shoulders to him. "You let everyone think it was me."

"I'm sorry," he muttered. "I didn't mean for anyone to be blamed. It smelt really bad. I was about to fess up when the underwear thing happened."

Gastrella's face turned fifty shades of red. "Now you are bringing that up again," she cried, running for the door.

"I'm sorry," Tanner yelled after her. His hands slapped against his sides. "I didn't mean to..."

She was gone.

Chapter Twenty-One

Gastrella took the long route to class. It was the only way to avoid seeing Tanner, at least before they had class together. She took the stairs two at a time, coming to an abrupt stop at the bottom.

"Hey," Molly said, avoiding eye contact.

"Hey," Gastrella replied, biting her upper lip. "You're wearing the hat. It looks good on you. How are you doing?"

"I'm getting better," Molly replied. "I wanted to apologize for what happened at my house. I should have been a better friend. I never even thanked you for the gift. I love it."

"I should have been here for you..."

"You couldn't have known," Molly blurted out. "Nobody did. I kept it to myself. I made a deal with the devil."

"What do you mean?" Gastrella asked.

"There was a reason why Cassidy didn't bother me before," Molly explained. "I set her up with my brother. The deal was as long as they were together, she left me alone. Tanner didn't even know."

Gastrella's eyes widened. "So when they broke up, you were fair game? That was all it took for her to treat you so poorly?"

"Not exactly," Molly replied. "As long as he was single, she didn't care. She still considered Tanner her property."

"So why?" Gastrella questioned.

"You still don't see it, do you?" Molly replied. "Tanner likes you. I mean, he really likes you."

"Alright," Gastrella said, pulling her books close to her chest. "I need to go to class. I'm tired of all the games."

Molly grabbed her shoulder. "Wait... I'm serious. That morning when you saw me by the fountain, Cassidy was warning me to make sure you and my brother never happened. She was jealous."

"There was nothing to be jealous of," Gastrella blurted out. "He picked up my pencil case when I dropped it."

"It was the way he looked at you," Molly explained. "Everyone else could see it. Anyway, that's why I told you to stay away from him at lunch. Then at the party, I could tell she was fuming you were there and that Tanner was talking to you. I literally saw my life flashing before my eyes."

"That's why you threw me under the bus..."

"Yeah," Molly admitted. "I knew you would bolt. That made Cassidy happy, for a bit. Then..."

"He stuck up for me," Gastrella said.

"Yeah," Molly replied. "I had no idea she took pictures of me that day. All the time she had spent not attacking me released at once. It spread like wildfire. I couldn't handle it... the stares... the comments." Her voice faded.

"I know," Gastrella said, taking a seat on the steps. "It sucks."

"I'm sorry," Molly offered. "I was so concerned about not having it happen to me, I didn't care if it happened to someone else. That was wrong."

"I get it," Gastrella admitted. "It shouldn't happen to anyone."

"Can you forgive me?" Molly asked.

Gastrella glanced up. "Yeah," she said. "If you can forgive me. We both made mistakes. Maybe we can start again."

Molly smiled. "Good plan. How about at Mrs. Natty's meeting after school? I'm required to go to them. It was part of the deal if I wanted to leave the hospital. They want to make sure I'm not going to do anything stupid."

Gastrella bit her lip. "I don't know..."

"You still mad at him?" Molly asked.

"A little," Gastrella admitted. "He threw me under the bus, too. If he actually likes me, why did he do that?"

"You telling me that your anxiety never made you do something you weren't proud of?" Molly asked. "He froze. He did stick up for you, though."

"Not about the stink he made!" Gastrella exclaimed.

Molly chuckled. "Was it that bad?"

"It was seriously ripe," Gastrella replied, laughing. "And everyone still thinks I was to blame."

"I know you like him," Molly teased. "It's a match made in the kitchen. Your first date can be a gourmet dinner of baked beans and cabbage. Then you can spend the rest of the night watching the stars and tooting."

"You're terrible," Gastrella said, laughing. The bell rang. "We better get to class. I'll see you at lunch."

"Talk to him," Molly said. "You two belong together."

"I'll think about it," Gastrella replied.

"Hey, how'd you know to get me a hat for my birthday?" Molly asked. "I never told anyone I collected hats."

"A good friend just knows these things," Gastrella replied, shrugging her shoulders. "Besides, you wear a different one every day."

Chapter Twenty-Two

"Are you going to tell me where we are going?" Gastrella asked.

"You'll see," Tanner replied, a sheepish grin crossing his lips. "It's a surprise." He opened the passenger door to his father's truck, offering her a hand up.

She held her breath, waiting for him to take his place beside her. The engine purred, offering momentary relief to the building tension. She'd never even had the nerve to imagine having a first date with anyone. Being with Tanner made it all that much better. She allowed herself a side glance at him. He returned the gesture, adding a wink. Her head snapped back forward, eyes fixed on the road.

She rubbed her hands, fingers intertwining as she fidgeted. It was all she could do to stop from biting her nails. In one snap, all of her efforts growing them would be lost. Once she bit one, the rest were sure to follow.

The radio blurted out garbled words mixed with songs as Tanner searched for a station. "Any preference?"

Gastrella shook her head, her anxiety hitting an all-time high. Inside, she cursed herself for not being able to speak. Her dry mouth simply wouldn't form any words. It wasn't as if they had only just met. They had been close friends for weeks without any apprehension. It was the label that made things awkward. Date was a four-letter word, especially to a girl who had never been on one.

"First stop!" Tanner exclaimed. He rounded the truck, offering her a hand down. "We need to pick up some supplies."

She alternated glances between her date and the grocery store. When he'd asked her out for dinner, she'd expected a restaurant. That alone was enough to send her stomach into knots.

Tanner grabbed a cart and pushed it from aisle to aisle, stopping to pick up a package of hot dogs and some buns. His brows rose and fell as he did a one-eighty, heading to the canned section. Her eyes widened, realizing what he was grabbing.

"You can't be serious!" Gastrella blurted out.

"What?" he replied. "Have you tried them before?"

"You know I don't eat things that cause..." Her words faded. She glanced around to see if anyone was nearby listening.

"Cause what?" Tanner asked, chuckling. His backside stuck out slightly as he pushed out a few putts from his butt.

"Oh no, you didn't!" Gastrella gasped.

He was already speed walking away. "Feel like some cheese?" he called back to her. "I brought a knife... we can cut some."

Not even biting her lip was going to stop a chuckle from escaping. Her feet moved as fast as they did while playing the same game with her brothers on grocery night. She caught up to him in the dairy section, almost wishing she'd stayed back a bit. Even her eyes stung from the fumes. "Phew!"

"Sorry," he said, a cheesy grin plastered on his face, appropriate for the situation. "We better get out of here before someone complains."

"Are you going to tell me where we are going?" Gastrella questioned.

"Patience," he replied.

*****

The truck rolled to a stop in the middle of a field. Tanner removed the keys from the ignition.

"We are here," he said, hopping out.

"Here, where?" Gastrella asked, jumping down before he made his way around the truck. The property was as beautiful as a well-kept park. Clumped together, several large trees loomed over the shore of a small lake beside them, rope swings dangling from their limbs.

"This is my family's summer house," he explained. "I thought we'd have a cookout." He held up a pair of long skewers and the wieners. "You mentioned you liked camping. I am rather fond of watching the sunset. I thought we'd eat and star gaze for a bit."

"Wieners and beans," she grimaced. "Do you have any idea what that will do to my stomach?"

He took her hands. "We both know the only reason you don't eat stuff like this is because you are afraid it will cause gas. I think we also both know you would love to try it."

"I don't want to," Gastrella started. "It would be embarrassing."

"Sh," he said. "I don't care if you fart. I know you don't want to in public, but when it is just the two of us, it's fine. I want you to feel comfortable when you are with me. Go ahead... let one rip."

"I don't have to," Gastrella replied.

"No, really," Tanner urged. "Fire the stink torpedo."

"I don't have to!" Gastrella exclaimed, laughing.

"I think most of your problem stems from worrying what would happen if you did," Tanner suggested. "I am not going to make fun of you."

"Of course I worry," Gastrella blurted out. "My name makes it twice as bad. Luckily, there are only a few more months to my birthday and I am going to change that."

"Are you sure?" Tanner questioned. "You shouldn't change your name because of what unimportant people think or say. It's the people who want to be with you for you that matter. I happen to like your name. It's different."

"Really?" Gastrella asked, raising her upper lip. "You don't think it's weird?"

"Yeah, it is," Tanner admitted. "But it's yours. I like you, Gastrella M. Balance, name and all." He cupped her chin in one hand, leaning forward. His lips brushed softly against hers. "Now, if there aren't any complaints, I'm going to make us dinner. There are blankets and pillows in the back of the truck if you are cold." He rubbed his hands together, preparing to build a fire in a stone pit. "Dinner will be served in twenty minutes."

Nothing could have wiped the grin from her face. In one evening, she finally understood. All her life, she'd been worried about those people who didn't matter in the greater scheme of things, instead of paying attention to the ones who did. She'd been responsible for a good portion of her own anxiety.

She chuckled watching Tanner hopping from side to side, trying to build as large a fire as he could. For the first time she felt relaxed enough to be herself. He brought that out in her. With no anxiety, her gas was non-existent. Even if she did have a burp from below, she felt secure enough to let it happen. That was exactly what she needed.

An orange glow reflected on the still surface of the lake. The sun was going down in a blaze of glory. She glanced up, a shooting star leaving a trail of glitter in the early evening sky.

Normally, she'd make a wish. At that moment, however, she decided someone else could use it more. She already had everything she wanted.

Author's Message

I hope you enjoyed reading Sometimes Love Stinks as much as I did writing it. I'd like to take a moment to discuss a serious topic... bullying.

In any form, mentally, physically or cyber-based, bullying another person or animal isn't acceptable. Most people are quick to agree with that statement, yet it continues to happen and, when it does, both sides of the equation need help.

The victims usually suffer in silence for many years. The effect on their psyche is profound, leaving scars they carry with them for the rest of their lives. In more severe cases, life can even be cut short because of one experience.

The ones doing the bullying tend to receive a slap on the hand rather than the counselling they need to solve deeper-rooted problems. They become victims of society itself.

Each of us can do our part by: reinforcing no tolerance rules; reaching out to those who might be involved in either role; and checking our own practices to make sure we are not engaging in such behaviour ourselves.

It's easy to snicker at someone's mismatched outfit without considering they can't afford anything else, or the overweight woman paying all her attention to an eclair, who is battling depression from losing her whole family in a car accident.

Is it human nature? I'd like to think otherwise. If you see someone in need, please offer a helping hand or words of advice. It can make more of a difference in someone's life than you could ever imagine. Help spread the magic.

Until next time...

Happy reading!

ABOUT THE AUTHOR

C.A. King is the recipient of several awards, including: The Hamilton Spectator Readers' Choice Award for 2017 & 2018 Best Local Author; The Brant News Readers' Choice Award for 2017 Best Local Author; Readers' Favorite award in the short story/novella category; the 2017 SIBA Award for Best New Adult; the 2017 SIBA Award for Best Novella; 2018 Readers' Favorite International Book Awards: Gold Medal in the Fiction - Supernatural genre; and 2018 Readers' Favorite International Book Awards: Bronze Medal in the Fiction - New Adult genre

Currently residing in Brantford, Ontario Canada, she lives with her two sons. She began her writing career after the tragic loss of her parents and husband. Redirecting her emotions through writing became therapeutic in her battle with depression and in 2014 she decided to publish some of her works.

Other Titles from C.A. King

The Portal Prophecies

These great titles in C.A. King's The Portal Prophecies series are available now at most online book retailers:

A Keeper's Destiny

A Halloween's Curse

Frost Bitten

Sleeping Sands

Deadly Perceptions

Finding Balance

Volume I (Books 1-3)

Volume II (Books 4-6)

The prophecies are the key to their survival. Can they solve them in time?

Shattering the Effects of Time

Join the Shinning brothers, Jessie, Dezi and Pete as they set out on a quest to save their younger sister. No magic known to them or their friends has ever been able to reverse the grip of time. A few legends, however, exist mentioning ancient items that may hold the key to do exactly that.

This brand new series will take you on a search for the Fountain of Youth and Mermaids; a quest for the Holy Grail; a trip to visit Daryl the mountain guru, in the hunt for the Cinamani Stone; on a search for Ambrosia, the food of the Gods; and other adventures.

Surviving the Sins: Answering the Call

The prophecies are being rewritten. This time someone is using the seven deadly sins: Lust; Gluttony; Greed; Sloth; Wrath; Envy; and Pride, to unlock an ancient evil. The book falls into Jade's hands to answer destiny's call. Can she survive the sins?

Surviving the Sins: Pride

No one is safe when a witch's pride is at stake.

Prudance is back in Pewterclaw, and she isn't about to give up her prestigious status without a fight - especially not because of vampires. As an eighth-generation witch, she plans to do whatever it takes to stop the proposed new legislation from becoming law, including waking the dead for help.

Humility isn't in her vocabulary. With an ego spinning out of control and ancestral power at her fingertips, Prudance weaves a plot to keep Jade and Gavin separated. Will it be enough to satisfy the spirits she summoned?

When her pride costs more than she bargained for, someone has to pay the tab - but who will it be?

Surviving the Sins: Lust

What Mother doesn't know won't hurt her.

Lucinda has spent her entire existence running The Organization and looking after Mother's needs without complaint. That's about to change. A burning desire had manifested inside her - one she could no longer deny... Lust.

When Constable Safron Black shows up unexpected with news of an imprisoned God, Lucinda unravels. With power fuelling her passion, she'll do anything to make Morynx her mate.

****

Jade and her friends find themselves at a standstill. They have already failed to stop Pride from completing its task and they haven't located any victims for the other six sins. A strange fire in the municipal office puts them hot on the trail of what could be answers. Will they be in time to stop the dial from moving and further opening the way for Morynx?

When Leaves Fall: A Different Point of View Story

Ralph wakes up to what others only experience in a nightmare. Chained to a shed, he has no idea where he is, or who his captor is. His memories a blurred at best. As the days press on he finds himself experiencing a roller coaster of feelings. Hunger, thirst and pain become his only companions. Flashbacks of a happier time are all he has to keep him going. As his situation deteriorates, he finds himself doubting the very things he wants most - a family.

When Leaves Fall is a dramatic-thriller with a twist. Keep the tissue box close for the ending.

Tomoiya's Story

A Vampire Tale. She had a secret but she wasn't the only one who had something to hide.

Book I ~ Escape to Darkness

Book II ~ Collecting Tears

Book III~ Coming Soon

Peach Coloured Daisies: A Cursed by the Gods Story

He couldn't die. An ancient curse meant she always did. This time, that was going to change - one way or another.

When Daisy's grandmother, her last living relative, passes away, she doesn't know where to turn. Things go from bad to worse when a local psychic tells her about a curse. Alone and confused, she ends up in front of her college professor's office, ready to cry her heart out in his arms.

Matt Demi might be the son of a God, but he's living the life of a cursed man. He's had to watch the woman he loves die on her twenty-first birthday countless times. Nothing he does seems to be able to affect the outcome. When she shows up at his office scared out of her wits by a psychic's prediction, he vows this time will be different.

With only three days, Matt will need to embrace a side of him he swore off long ago to save her, but will he lose himself in the process?

Flower Shields: A Four Horsemen Novel

Meet the four horsemen: Michael, Gabrielle, Uriel and Raphael. For centuries their job has been to guard the gates of hell, making sure they never open. Without the keys, there was never any real threat. That's about to change. There are rumours on the horizon that demon followers unearthed scrolls that explain exactly how to find the lost keys. This new battle is a race to see which side locates them first.

Michael couldn't care less about the love story behind how and why the world was created. In fact, nothing matters to him other than keeping the gates to hell closed. If one of the lost keys ever fell into the wrong hands, all humanity would be doomed. He's not going to let that happen - at any cost.

****

Tara's life is nothing short of a disaster. She's managed to flunk out of college with about the same amount of dignity as every relationship she's been in. The only constant in her life has been her love for flowers. When she's attacked at work, a stranger comes to her aid. Michael might be good-looking, but he's also arrogant, bossy and crazy. He's also her only chance to figure out who attacked her and why. Should she follow her heart and trust him - or listen to her head and run?

Drawing Strength From Words: A Four Horsemen Novel

Meet the four horsemen: Michael, Gabrielle, Uriel and Raphael.

For centuries their sole purpose has been guarding the sealed gates to hell. Without keys, there was never any real threat. That was about to change...

For Gabrielle, protecting mankind was merely a job for which she received little credit. The vast insecurities of men altered history itself, portraying her as a masculine brute. Taking a back seat to her brothers seemed the right thing to do, but left a bitter taste in her mouth and an impenetrable barricade shielding her heart.

****

Ryder bounced around the system from the moment both his parents were killed. Between that and run-ins with the law for crimes he never committed, it seemed the whole world was conspiring against him. Never growing attached to anyone was rule number one: a rule he'd never broken until a white-haired vixen, with blocks of ice on her shoulders, walked right into his life. Melting through those frosty layers became all that mattered, even if that meant sacrificing himself in the process.

Miracles Not Included

A heartfelt romantic story about: life; love; loss; and learning to love again. If only life came with instructions and a warning label ~ Miracles Not Included.

****

Chris was born to be a writer. Even the smallest of details couldn't pass without notice, often becoming part of a plot for her next novel. The one thing she never saw coming was her husband's sudden illness.

Jason loved his wife from the moment they met. Nothing could ever change that - nothing except the death sentence he'd been handed - a terminal cancer diagnosis.

His story was ending: Hers was starting a new chapter and more than one miracle was needed to turn the page.

Twisted Tales of a Dead End Street

A paranormal mystery laced with comedic undertones: Twisted Tales of a Dead End Street.

Nine neighbours were invited to the mysterious dinner party at 9 Nine Street. Their host, the owner of the mansion, had more planned for the evening than just roast beef.

When the secret of their quiet street was revealed, everything changed, blurring the lines between the tangible and the paranormal.

Was the number nine the difference between life and death? Would any of them survive long enough to uncover the truth? They would each soon find out this wasn't a simple case of who-done-it so much as one of what was being done and by whom.

Shot Through The Heart: A Faerie Tale

A tale of two worlds - one filled with magic; the other void of it. But what happened to those trapped between the two? Adelia was about to find out...

Magic and structure were the foundations of her existence. Temptation controlled the ability to destroy everything she knew. The world of men held a powerful allure over her heart, waking that which had long been dormant. It enticed her, snagging her in a web of emotions.

A decision had to be made. Was feeling love for the first time worth sacrificing magic and immortality?

Truly Unfortunate

Growing up in Knoll County wasn't easy, especially without any childhood memories. Truly spent her whole life searching for the answers her mind refused to reveal. There might have been horrors in her past, but her current existence wasn't much better than a nightmare. After beginning treatments with a new doctor, disturbing visions began to resurface. The stench of death surrounded her, but where exactly was it coming from?

Jeff always knew he wanted to be one of Knoll County's finest and had no problem achieving that dream. A part of his ambition stemmed from the death of a classmate at the tender age of nine. It might have been ruled an accident, but his gut told him otherwise. When people start turning up dead in the same pattern, Jeff will be forced to put everything on the line to connect the dots between past and present. But in doing so, will his own future be jeopardized?

Truly Unfortunate is a dark paranormal thriller that will leave readers with chills after answering the question: Which is stronger... the boundaries of reality or the safety on one's own mind?

www.ingramcontent.com/pod-product-compliance
Lightning Source LLC
Chambersburg PA
CBHW052139170626
46812CB00004B/1506